# _A_ Statute _with_ Limitations

## Before #MeToo

BECKY STARR

HUMAN RITES

ISBN-10 0-692-17568-2
ISBN-13 978-0-692-17568-2

Printed in the United States of America

To contact the author:
www.astatutewithlimitations.com

Characters, motives and scenes have been fictionalized to achieve literary effect, and should not be taken as factual. *A Statute with Limitations: Before #MeToo* is a work of fiction. While the struggle to end sexual abuse by therapists did actually occur in the 1980's, this novel is not to be taken as a factual representation of persons, events, motives, businesses, or institutions of that time period. Any resemblance to such is either coincidental or used fictitiously for the author's creative purposes.

*In gratitude to all who have helped me*
*complete this project.*

# *Prologue*

Certainly amnesty cannot be viewed as justice if we think of justice only as retributive and punitive in nature. We believe however that there is another kind of justice—a restorative justice which is concerned not so much with punishment as with correcting imbalances, restoring broken relationships...with healing, harmony and reconciliation. Such justice focuses on the experience of victims; hence the importance of reparation.

—Desmond Tutu,
South African Truth and Reconciliation
Commission, 6, p.1

# 1

Humans appear hard-wired to pursue justice. Children in the tribunal of the playground are quick to shout, "It's not fair." Demonstrators gather outside of government buildings to demand it. Attorneys petition the highest court, the wisest in the land, to discern what is just and fair. Even the God humans create is imagined as a Judge supremely omniscient, rewarding good and punishing the wicked.

Let me introduce myself and my role. My name is Themis, Greek goddess, by occupation tasked since the beginning of time to oversee the advance of human justice. One hiccup—I can only observe, never intervene, which accounts for my ulcers. Given that humans have heart, head, and free will, I find their progress quite mystifying and befuddling.

There have been stellar moments in human progress that I do brag about to my colleagues. Love that Solomon, so creative in resolving conflict. And Desmond Tutu, thumbs up. But across time, good people, innocent people, have been crucified, enslaved, or incarcerated, while powerful people commit heinous crimes with impunity. Not so good, they remind me.

I have a counterpart and compatriot, a Roman goddesses named Justice (would you believe?). The two of us don't always agree. I have to excuse her, though, she's been blindfolded by humans since the Age of Reason. While I envision the scale of justice as a balanced approach between heart and head, she relies heavily on law and tradition. That causes some chaos in our relationship!

We're overseeing some events surfacing in 1980's—in your time. A woman named Carole Thornton is struggling to find a very elusive justice. I'm betting she will triumph; Justice does not agree with me. This is what we watch unfold.

# 2

**October, 1982**

Attorney Abe Friedman poses a final question to his star witness in the State's case against the psychiatrist, Dr. Harry Jansen. He thinks Carole deserves a chance to speak her piece after what that jerk has put her through.

"Ms. Thornton, is there anything you want to say to Dr. Jansen?"

*Finally. My chance to speak freely to the man whose lies have caused me so much unnecessary distress.* Carole leans forward. She looks directly at the accused. "I **dare** you to look me in the eye and say this never happened."

The click-click-click of the court reporter comes to a halt. Silence hangs heavy in the room as all wait for his response.

# 3

**February, 1981**

"Jake"

No answer.

Betty glances at her watch, raises her voice. "Jake, you have a half hour to get dressed and get the kids to school. I fed them but I have to leave. I have an early meeting at work."

He stirs, rolls over, opens one wary eye.

Now that she has his attention, she adds more to his discontent. "I may be a bit late coming home."

"So what's new?"

Ignoring the sarcastic tone in Jake's muffled voice, Betty continues. "The med students are starting their psych rotations. I have to meet with each one of them today. It's very time consuming. Please, please, please remember to pick up the kids and feed them?"

"Yeah, sure," Jake mumbles, flips back over and pulls the comforter over his head. Another day wasted at home when he should be at work.

He never planned to be a stay-at-home nanny when he married Betty, both with respectable careers and high hopes for a bright future together. The current situation doesn't fit that vision.

He hates being stuck in the Rust Belt when his own plant moved south, but she won't consider a move. This town may work for her career, but not for his. Manufacturing is never moving back here.

Some people drink when they're depressed. Jake sleeps. It's gotten to be a bad habit.

Eventually he drags himself up and slips into the jeans and sweatshirt he tossed on the floor last night No need to shower or shave. Who at the local McDonald's really cares what he looks like? It's become his morning hangout where he's about as significant as the trash folks ditch as they leave the place.

He makes his way to the open window just in time to catch Betty, who's out on the driveway by now.

"How late do you expect to be tonight?" Jake calls out.

"Don't know. Students don't always arrive on time. First day they tend to get lost in the place."

"Aren't YOU the boss? If you *made* them show up on time, maybe you'd have some time left for me and the kids."

"We've had this discussion before, Jake. Knock off the whining. Do we really have to share our issues with the neighbors?"

Betty slams the garage door and jumps into her Volkswagen Rabbit.

"Men." Betty mutters as she heads out. "Maybe I'd be more in a rush to get home if I didn't always find you sleeping on the couch."

Now free to air her growing frustration without any backlash, she continues her rant. "Damn it, Jake. You like my income. It pays the mortgage. But not my long hours? I have to do my job twice as well as the men around me. The least sign of weakness on my part . . . there'd be ten men waiting in line to steal my position."

By the time the physician's VW reaches the third stop-and-go light, a transformation takes over. Betty relegates home and family to the back seat as wife and mother morph into Elizabeth Schubachs, PhD, M.D. who has an important position at the County Mental Health Center.

# 4

It's the 1980's. No more long-term institutional care for the mentally ill. No more locking the door and throwing away the keys. President Reagan has new funding priorities. Grants, like hers, are awarded to innovative programs that promise speedy and permanent recovery. The experimental approach she's engaged in, referred to as building a *therapeutic community,* is designed specifically for the treatment of highly functioning patients. One of her responsibilities is to introduce incoming med students to an approach that promises to reduce recidivism in this specific patient population.

She's overseen three student rotations in the past year. Based on those experiences, Schubachs anticipates boredom. Students, she's observed, regard this phase of their training as a *vacation* from the real world of medicine. Their lack of enthusiasm is rubbing off on her. She wants to light a fire under them but that's hard to do when her own enthusiasm barely flickers.

Upon arriving at the Center, Schubachs sees her colleague exiting his Cadillac. She grabs her coat, coffee and briefcase, and vacates her car in a rush.

"Morning, Jerry," she calls out. "Ready for our new bunch of students?"

"Not my job anymore," he chuckles. "I put in my time. Your turn now."

Peale holds the door open for Betty. "You've got a bit to manage there."

"You can say that again," she mutters.

"Well, have a good day," he offers as they move in opposite directions down the circular halls.

"Thanks. You, too. It's gonna be a long one."

Betty likes Dr. Peale but she doesn't appreciate how he treats her like his little sister instead of a colleague. She's always felt a definite tension in their professional partnership. Today is no different.

Six months earlier, in compliance with new affirmative action guidelines, the department chair hired a woman to share leadership on the project. His boss made a peculiar comment at the time. "For reasons I'm not free to disclose, we want this woman on the staff of the Medical College. She'll be partnering with you."

Peale knew better than to ask for an explanation. Her hiring sounded personal. He hoped she wasn't a feminist out to prove she could make it in a man's world. No way he wanted to get pulled into *that* game.

"I'll teach her the ropes," he promised his boss. "If she fails, it won't be for lack of adequate supervision."

Out of curiosity, Peale vetted her, concluded she might actually have the balls for the job. Not only had Elizabeth Schubachs graduated with top honors in her class, she had applied for and been accepted for a professorship at the Medical College very shortly thereafter. Her years of university teaching in a nursing program combined with a recently acquired physician's license with a specialty in psychiatry, made her well qualified for her current position.

"Fine. She fits in fine." Peale assured their supervisor at the six-month review. "She's not the fuzzy social worker type. She's tough, like we need to be at County. She'd never fit in at the private sanitarium down the road where they coddle their patients, but she's perfect here. Professional, cool, almost cold at times."

"Is that good or bad?" his boss inquired.

"In this kind of work, it's good. We're not a mental health spa," Peale said, a tone of derision in his voice. "We get society's hard-core dropouts."

"Hmm. A bit cynical?"

"Our patients are dumped here by the police who don't know what else to do with them. Or hauled in by family members desperate for relief."

Peale modified his tone when he saw a critical look cross his superior's face. "I admit *some* patients are looking to find solutions to some tough situations but many have just given up."

"So. We're more than the dumping ground you first suggested," his boss responded.

"You've *got* to shrug off their problems once you leave the office. Dr. Schubachs can do that."

"Good. Good. The grant report is coming due. Any way she can help out? Is there something she could do so you can focus on that?"

Peale mulled over his superior's suggestion before answering. He hesitated to admit he hated supervising med students. Their attitudes were draining.

To this quick-fix generation, psychiatry is less than engaging. As a medical discipline, it rests at the bottom of the totem pole. Probably always will, until something truly horrific wakes people up to the importance of treating mental illness.

Peale came to a decision. "How about letting Schubachs take over student supervision?"

"Too boring?"

Measuring his words carefully so as not to irritate his boss, he explained, "Students don't see much progress during the six weeks they spend on the unit. It's too short a stint to build a therapeutic relationship. They chart a few intake notes, take a stab at diagnosis, and experiment with prescribing appropriate psychotropic drugs. Under supervision, of course."

"Not nearly as exciting as resuscitating a patient in the throes of a fatal heart attack. Or as rewarding as delivering a newborn. I get that,

Jerome. So we'll give you a break. Let Schubachs supervise the students. See how she does."

# 5

Schubachs drops off her belongings at her office. Today being Monday, she takes an underground passage to the emergency admission unit, where she will select from incoming patients those who might do well in a therapeutic community.

She notices a mouse scurry along the damp concrete walls of the old tunnel. Its erratic behavior reminds her of rats caught in a laboratory maze. One or two eventually find a way out; most give up exhausted in a futile search. This one seems to be one of those, just going round and round in circles.

At the tunnel's end, Schubachs takes the elevator to the 8th floor. She manages a weak smile for the security guard, who recognizes her, opens the door, then locks it securely behind her.

"Morning, Dr. Schubachs," a male nurse sighs wearily. "Am I glad to see you! Must be a full moon. Brings out all the loonies. We're way over capacity."

"Great," she mumbles.

"Hi, Doc," nurse practitioner Alice Marshall calls out. "It's a zoo."

"So I hear."

Schubachs settles into the well-worn government-issued chair. She glances quickly through intake notes trying to ignore a red-headed man pacing up and down the hall outside the nursing station, blaring out Irish shanties at the top of his lungs.

"I can't concentrate," Schubachs complains. "I see Mike's back. What happened this time?"

"Same ole, same ole. Went off his meds, got drunk. Flying higher than a kite. Want him back on your unit?"

"Not 'til he sobers up. Get him back on his meds first. We don't need that racket to get the others riled up."

"It's been like homecoming week without the celebration," Marshall continues. "Lance got into another bar fight. Sandra's been threatening people."

"So much for recidivism," Schubachs sighs. "Back to the unit with both of them."

"Lock the place?"

"Temporarily for sure. Get the transfers over by 10:30. The community will determine if we need to keep the door locked."

"Three newbies arrived late last night that you might like to consider for your project."

"Ok, let's hear about them. Man, it's hard to concentrate with Mike screaming in my ears."

"Try six hours of that," Marshall mumbles.

Schubachs raises an eyebrow. "Isn't that what you're getting paid for?"

"Okay. Business." The nurse summarizes her observations. "35 year old female, white, married, three children, homemaker. Three month old twins. Depressed. 19 year old white female—ER referral after treatment for malnutrition and dehydration. Looks like someone from Auschwitz, if you ask me. 42 year old female, white, married with three children, works as a part-time psych aide while completing her Master's degree.

"What's *she* doing here? That last one?"

"Carole Thornton? Insisted on being admitted. Threatened her former psychiatrist. Said she'd commit suicide and leave her body on his front lawn if he didn't help her. He called it in. I'd never dare threaten a doctor like that!"

"A borderline would."

The nurse continues, "Her tank top reads *Fragile: Handle with Care.* That's her message to the world, I guess. She lost 75 pounds recently, had lengthy stays at two different psych hospitals recently. In between, she lived in a group home."

Schubachs reads the rest of Thornton's admission notes out loud.

"Entered a convent at age 13. Reports marriage issues. Filed for a divorce but dropped it. Claims she was sent back home from her last hospital when her insurance company delayed payment. Patient reports sexual activity with two former therapists."

"*WHAT?*"

In a very uncharacteristic move Dr. Schubachs slams the admission chart shut.

Marshall suggests "Maybe she fantasized that?"

"I'll know better after I talk to her. What's your gut reaction to her?"

"More together than our typical patient. Depressed, anxious, confused, maybe. But psychotic? Uh-uh. Been up playing canasta with Lance and Sandy all night."

"Set up a room where I can talk to her in private. Not sure this is the best place for her."

"By the way, she's a cutter. When the orderlies did their search last night, they discovered recent scars on her wrists. She brought along antidepressants and anti-anxiety meds."

"Let's see."

Marshall opens the locked cupboard and draws out the tray with Carole's drugs—Elavil and Xanax. The nurse hands them to Schubachs for official identification.

"Send them to the pharmacy. Now, the room?"

Marshall sends an orderly to find a vacant room where Dr. Schubachs can interview Carole.

"Room 810," he suggests, upon returning.

"Take her there. I'll be in shortly."

Dr. Schubachs leaves the nursing station, glad to put distance between herself and Manic Mike who continues to trumpet Irish shanties in the hallway.

The orderly escorts Carole to Room 810. "Have a seat, Mrs. Thornton," he tells her.

The patient takes her place on the other side of a gray metal table opposite a rather plain-looking woman who appears to be in her late thirties, maybe early forties. The woman's dark hair is kept in an easy-to-care-for bob. She has brown eyes, a grim face, black oxford shoes, and a cotton shirt-waist dress. The woman appears to Carole to be an aide or a social worker of some kind.

Carole rubs the lucky Wonder Woman pendant between her thumb and her finger. She managed to get it past the orderlies during the strip search even though they roamed over every inch of her body, like women checking out produce they're about to devour. Not a pleasant experience.

"I thought I was going to see a *doctor.*" Carole's face registers disappointment.

"I am the doctor. My name is Dr. Schubachs."

"Sorry," Carol apologizes. "Not used to female psychiatrists."

Schubachs ignores the patient's *faux pas.* "I see you admitted yourself around 11:30 last night. Why?"

"County is the only hospital left for me. I can't see Dr. Orlanski anymore. I work as a psychiatric aide at the hospital where he practices. The staff is uncomfortable with an employee being a patient there. It exposes their own vulnerability. I guess they think it's not good for the patients."

"What about your other therapist? Dr. Mielke, the one who just discharged you from your second hospital?"

"Good riddance. He's vacationing in the Bahamas. I knew his therapy wouldn't work as soon as I walked in his office. Pfff...a bust of Sigmund Freud on his desk, even wears a Freudian-style beard. He just dubbed me an *hysterical* woman from the get-go."

"Are you...hysterical?"

"I guess I can be when I am desperate. When you learn my psychiatric history, maybe you'll understand why."

"I'm most curious about your claim that two previous therapists engaged in sexual activity as part of therapy. Tell me about that?"

"Well." Carole pauses. "Please try to understand," she pleads. "I was in the convent from age 13 to age 23. When I left I was totally naive about so many things, especially about sex. It was a very confusing time for me. The transition...was hard."

Carole checks Dr. Schubachs' face, but this therapist is hard to read. She continues trying to explain her situation back then, hoping she'll understand. "I wanted to be a normal human being. I wasn't. I was emotionally crippled. I planned to return to the convent eventually. Someone had to fix me or I wouldn't be able to help others. A nun psychologist named Sister Amelia referred me to him. Said he would help. He didn't."

Carole squirms. The room suddenly seems too hot.

"You gave up your plan to return to the convent?"

"How could I ever be a Bride of Christ after having sex with the doctor?" Carole flushes, stares at the floor.

"I got married instead." Her voice registers both pain and regret. "What other choice did I have?"

"The report states you lost 75 pounds in the past year. Is that true?" Schubachs asks Carol.

"Yes."

"Intentional?"

"Nope. I mean I didn't go on a diet or anything like that. I did a lot of walking trying to sort things out. The pounds just came off." She pauses before adding, " I know. I look like my father now. We're about the same weight now. He's in treatment for pancreatic cancer, though. I'm not."

"And the second therapist who engaged in sex with you? Tell me about him?"

"It's a her. She's the nun. I'm still trying to make sense of what she did."

Carole doesn't want to say any more about these two relationships. She skillfully shifts the topic to something more positive. "I'm in graduate school. Working on my master's degree."

"Hmm...what's your major?"

"Adult education. My degree will be in Administrative Leadership with a focus on women's studies."

"What prompted you to go back to school?"

"If I get a degree, I might be able to support my kids. I won't feel so...inadequate. It might even give my life purpose."

"Are you sure you belong in this facility, Carole? Why don't you go to some private hospital?"

Carole sighs, a bit disheartened. County is her last hope. This is exactly where she belongs. If she can't find an answer here, she'll...

"I'm waiting for an answer," Dr. Schubachs says.

"I can't go back to Dr. Orlanski's hospital. My second hospitalization was a total disaster. I started cutting myself there. I never did that before." Carole twists her wrists downward to hide the scars.

"Do you know why you did that?" Dr. Schubachs inquires.

"It was a Catholic hospital. It felt like the convent as soon as I walked through the door," she recalls. "When they took away normal eating utensils and gave us plastic knives, I just rebelled. I can do as much damage with a plastic knife as any other if that's what I want to do. I wanted to show them I was in charge of my life, not them. They *really* got angry about that."

"Do you still do that, cut yourself?"

"Sometimes—when I hurt a lot inside. Cutting helps me let off steam when things are building out of control inside. It keeps me from doing something much worse. I don't cut myself in places people can see it anymore. I don't like people getting all upset."

"I hope you won't feel it necessary to do that anymore."

"I hope so, too."

Dr. Schubachs asks again, "Do you really want to stay here?"

"This *is* where I belong. I know people consider County the bottom of the barrel. That's right where I am now. I'm afraid I will commit suicide out there. I don't want to do that. I want to get better. I love my kids. I want to be able to take care of them." A single tear makes its way down her cheek.

"You don't seem suicidal right now. What happened to change that?" Dr. Schubachs asks.

"I think someone here will be able to help me." Carole's voice trails off. "Can you help me, *please?*"

"I'm going to assign you to my caseload. You'll be transferred to an open unit in a little while. It's a teaching unit. We have group meetings every morning. As many as thirty to thirty-five people attend—medical students, interns, psychology students, occupational therapists, nurses, aides. Patients as well," she adds as if they're an afterthought.

"So we're sort of on display?" Carole interjects.

The doctor ignores that remark. "Two psychiatrists, Dr. Peale and I conduct the group. Do you think you can handle that?"

"I like group work." Carole's face reflects interest.

"I'll be seeing you privately twice a week, too."

"How soon can I go? It's a little crazy in this place. I worked on an admission unit but it wasn't as crazy as this one. Not even when we were admitting Hippies in the 60's."

"Just so you know, the open door policy changes with new admissions, or when patients are in crisis and need tighter security. The community votes on whether to keep the door locked or unlocked."

"You use peer pressure?" Carole asks.

"We regard it as peer support," the psychiatrist corrects.

"When will I see you next?" Carole says, eager to begin treatment. "Soon, I hope."

"I'll see you up on the unit later this morning," Dr. Schubachs says as she begins writing. "Now I have some notes to finish. Just let yourself out."

Carole gets up to leave. "Thanks."

# 6

She returns to the admission unit with a new purpose to her step. There she gathers her belongings to prepare for the transfer, packing a large dose of hope in with her meager belongings.

Mentally she begins to explain the state she was in when she first left the convent to her new therapist. Could Dr. Schubachs ever understand what that was like?

*When the convent door closed behind me, I felt the summer breeze massaging my bare legs and fingering my hair, something I hadn't felt in years.*

*My sister picked me up, drove me to her suburban home. Her Cape Cod seemed like a doll house after the ten years I'd spent in institutional living. Physical space wasn't all that was strange and different.*

*We talked during supper! At her table, my soul was nourished by human conversation instead of spiritual reading. Giggles were welcome as the kids were tucked in for the night. No one imposed a canonical Great Silence for the next twelve hours. As the household settled down a black and white TV brought the day's news into focus. I was no longer isolated from the world I lived in.*

*As I fell asleep on a makeshift cot set up in the living room, I wondered if I'd ever find the self I seemed to have lost in those convent years. Since my dream of being a nun was now tossed asunder, where did I fit in? Though I got my state ID the next day, I had a long way to go in my search for a new identity.*

*At the tender age of twelve, I had been lured by religious propaganda into a cloistered life. We were robbed of a normal adolescence there, many developmental tasks left unfinished. I now faced a crash course in growing up.*

*For the first time I had money to manage. I set up my first banking account, applied for my first paid job, got my first paycheck, wrote my first check.*

*I planned my daily schedule instead of following one Sister Superior dictated.*

*I went shopping. I bought clothes instead of sewing a habit from black woolen serge. I experimented with styling my now-exposed hair.*

*I rubbed elbows with unfamiliar people. Men were now a part of my life. I struggled with co-ed socializing, like dancing and playing volleyball, but was no good at either. I went on my first date unsure of what to expect. What should I say? What should I do?*

*Alienated from family for many years, I wasn't sure how to reconnect.*

*I rode public transportation to work until I saved enough to purchase a car. I took driving lessons, obtained a license, and began driving my second-hand Ford Fairlane.*

*My former order no longer welcomed me on their campus. I had become a persona non grata, tossed aside like broken pottery. They insisted I transfer to a new college to finish my senior year, which I did. I expected my grades to go down as I competed in a co-ed college, but surprisingly, they went up, and I treasured the new-found academic freedom.*

*I needed a trustworthy, experienced hand to guide me through the maze. I thought Dr. Jansen would do that. I pinned my hopes on him.*

# 7

"Wait here," the orderly tells Carole upon their arrival at the new unit. "Gotta check you in. You can keep most of your belongings, but not sharps. They'll be stored in the nursing station."

Having worked in the admissions unit of a private mental hospital, and having been admitted to two other facilities recently, Carole is familiar with the routine. She's experienced *One Flew Over the Cuckoo's' Nest* from both sides of the thick glass window that enshrines the nursing station. She knows a glass cage, a uniform, and a set of keys is all that really separates *us* from *them*.

Eventually a female aide comes out to introduce herself. "We'd better hurry. I have only a few minutes to show you your bedroom before group starts. You'll be sharing the room with Angela."

The two of them head to the farthest end of a long hallway, to a room totally removed from sight of the nurses' station. Carole suspects a lot of shenanigans could go unnoticed in this part of the unit.

"Yours is the sofa bed near the window; Angela's is near the bathroom," the aide says. "You can put your clothes in there," she adds as she gestures to a wooden wardrobe, and then turns to leave. She calls back over her shoulder, "Be sure to watch the time. You're expected to show up for group on your own. There won't be a bell or any other signal."

Carole observes the room is not unlike the one she vacated just over a month ago. Both hospital rooms are furnished with sofas that convert into a bed at night. Both have a desk, a chair, a wastebasket, a small dresser, and a lamp. Clean but simple. Enough for a temporary stay. She quickly unpacks and heads for group.

Over half of the seats are filled by the time Carole arrives in a room large enough to hold thirty or forty participants. Most are in street clothes, making it difficult to sort out patients from staff. Except for the keys. She looks around the circle and spots Lance's familiar face. His face and stoic demeanor remind Carole of the stately Native American captured on the buffalo nickel. She takes the empty chair next to his.

"Glad to see someone I know," she comments.

"Figured you'd end up here. What'ya think of the place?"

"Not too shabby," she says. "Tons better than the admission unit. Even a colored TV in the living room. Should be easy for the staff to keep tabs on us with the wide open spaces." She pauses, then adds, "Except in the bedroom area. Anything out of line is gonna happen there."

"So who's in the cage? Us or them?" He chuckles as he gestures toward the nursing station, still visible through the wide open door.

"Good question, Lance. I'd say we're all in the Cuckoo's Nest!"

"Remember Nurse Ratched was kookier than any of the patients. The aids here are much nicer, and a bit saner."

Carole whispers to Lance, "I see Sandy. She looks nice, pretty actually, in street clothes. She seems to be on very familiar terms with the staff."

"She's been here a lot," Lance whispers back. "Sandy's a tough one to live with. Smart. Great as a friend but don't ever cross her." Then he adds by way of explanation, "She's the daughter of a survivor from the camps." Carole catalogs his caution for future reference. She then searches for the manic red-headed singer of Irish shanties who's nowhere to be seen. "Don't see Mike. Maybe we'll get to sleep tonight."

Their chatter ends when Dr. Peale arrives and takes a seat. He introduces himself and other staff members to the new class of med students that is drifting in. As a newcomer, Carole chooses to listen and observe rather than talk. By the next day, ready or not, she will become a much more significant player in the group.

Retreating to her room after group, Carole meets her roommate Angela, who is strikingly beautiful with her ebony eyes, well-manicured nails, and carefully plaited dreadlocks. She talks to people not present in the room, laughs at unspoken jokes, and sings softly to herself. Carole likens her to Ophelia in Shakespeare's *Hamlet*: great beauty marred by mental illness, seeking refuge from pain in an imaginary world of her own creation.

When Carole crawls into bed early that evening, she falls into a restful sleep. With the staff around to protect her, she feels secured against the nightmarish impulses to harm herself. Not long afterwards she wakes, startled.

*Something's wrong! Someone's in the room who doesn't belong.*

Carole makes out the figure of a man hovering over Angela. Groans and moans suggest sexual activity. Angela at first glance seems to be a somewhat willing participant. But her giggles, a characteristic language in a schizophrenic world, suggest perhaps a heightened level of anxiety.

Carol freezes in place. Her mind races wildly. *Who is this person? What should I do? WHERE IS THE STAFF?*

Finally the bedroom door crashes opens. Two large men enter, flashlights searching the dark room.

"Franklin!" an orderly commands. "Get the Hell off of her, you creep!" Amidst sounds of scuffling and cursing, the two uniformed men yank Franklin off the bed, handcuff him, and drag him from the room. "Finally, caught you in the act," the other orderly says. "This is going to cost you. Big time," he warns.

Moments later, a visibly shaken nurse arrives. She wraps a blanket around Angela, then escorts her from the room. "Hush, quiet down. You'll wake the other patients," the nurse cautions, as she reaches to close the door behind her. "You're okay now. We have things to talk about."

Almost as an afterthought, she calls out to Carole who is still huddled under her blanket, "Go back to sleep. It's okay now."

But it's not!

Sleep is now impossible. Her heart throbs in rapid beat with her racing thoughts. She questions why she didn't go for help, why didn't she lift a finger to stop what was going on? She wonders if this was rape? Part of her says NO. Rape is a violent, forcible act—at least that's how it is shown in movies. Besides, rape victims fight back. Angela never resisted. On the other hand, could she really consent when she lives in a different world? Something about this feels like rape.

She questions why she ever thought this was a safe place. That's as much an illusion as the ones Angela creates.

To relieve her mounting anxiety, Carole reaches for the Wonder Woman pendant around her neck, the one her mother gave her so long ago. She had a habit of fingering it whenever she heard a fight break out between Mom and Dad. Its magic doesn't work any better now than it did back then.

She needs something to distract her. She remembers she has an unfinished assignment for her Lifelong Learning class. She could work on that. The assignment is to describe an event in her childhood that foreshadows the woman she wants to become.

"I fantasized I would become a Wonder Woman of sorts who would fight off the forces of evil around me. Somehow that image doesn't jive with my current situation," Carole mutters as she begins a rough draft.

*The bombing of Pearl Harbor on December 7, 1941 set my mom into labor. She returned from the hospital the next day still pregnant.*

*By the time I was born a week later, Congress had declared war on Japan, the Axis had declared war on the United States, and World War II was in full swing. Mom says my infant asthma was so pronounced she thought I would die. I probably found it difficult to breathe in an atmosphere so thick with fear, and with my father's smoking. He assured her I would live. He saw a great deal of fight in my eyes.*

*During the next decade of world-wide fear and chaos, comic book writers created superheroes with superhuman powers who could destroy archvillains. As I grew older, when I felt an asthma attack coming on, I latched on to those strong enforcers of law and order to escape the anxiety I detected in adults around me. They worried constantly about rationing, family members sent off to the war, and air raids. I so wished I could be a superhero.*

*But I was also cradled in the hope and determination of my parents' Greatest Generation of real superheroes who would eventually rescue and rebuild a war-torn world . . .*

# 8

Carole approaches group the next morning groggy as a new-born kitten. When she enters the room, she sees Irish Shanty Mike, finally sober and back on his meds, now chatting with Lance. She joins them.

"I'm Carole. You must be Mike. I heard you singing on the admission unit."

"Ouch. Caught me at my worst."

"Forget it, Mike," she says. "We all have our days."

"Yep, the black sheep returns," Mike says with a grin. "I missed you guys," he says to Lance.

"Hey, Carole, we're trying to figure out what's going on," Lance interrupts. "Quite a commotion last night. And the unit is locked this morning. Mike saw Franklin in handcuffs. I hope the guy didn't blow it again."

"What do you mean?" Carole asks.

"All three of us were charged with misdemeanors. Mike, drunk and disorderly; me, assault in a bar fight; Franklin, stalked the wrong woman, and she reported him to the cops. Same judge ordered us to spend time in jail or come out here to get our heads straightened out. We all chose this place. Food's better." Lance chuckles.

"Wonder what Franklin did," Mike says. "Hope he didn't go after Angela. He has the hots for her. I told him to cool it," Mike recounts. "Bet he didn't listen."

About then, a disheveled Dr. Peale arrives and calls the group to order.

"Wow, he looks washed out," Lance whispers.

In a disheartened voice, the psychiatrist announces the day's agenda. "I'm sure you're all wondering about the disturbance on the unit last night. I suspect rumors are rampant. Rumors aren't good for anyone, especially not in the open community here. Dr. Schubachs and I think you have a right to facts, instead of rumors."

"You also have a right to feel safe here," Dr. Schubachs adds, glancing in Carole's direction.

"Franklin is about to join us," Dr. Peale continues. "I want him to take responsibility for what he did to Angela last night."

"Told you," Mike whispers.

Accompanied by two officers, Franklin saunters in and takes a seat.

"Franklin, most of us know why you're here. The court gave you a chance to get help instead of jail time. You just blew it." Dr. Peale pauses to let his message sink in.

Sandra, who understands the trauma of losing family better than most people in the room, jumps in to defend Franklin. "He never gets company, you know. He told me his mama's dead and his old man's in prison for shooting her. Said he was too young to remember but his grandma told him."

"Shut up, bitch," Franklin mutters.

Dr. Peale slips into the role of a disappointed father correcting an errant son. "Franklin, don't you get it? What you did to Angela last night is statutory rape."

Franklin's eyes are bulging now. "Statutory rape? Whatcha mean? Watz that?"

"Angela's doesn't know what she's doing half the time. You went for her because she's easy, and you know it."

Franklin grins. "I like her, she likes me. Man, what's wrong with that? Lotta women like me. I wanted to have some fun. Nothin' wrong with that!"

"A mental hospital is not the place for that," the psychiatrist informs him. "You were warned, many times. Right in this room. Now you just added a rape charge to your other offenses."

"Statutory rape," he mutters. "Never heard of such a thing." Franklin remains sullen, champing on a wad of bubble gum. He burps loudly. No one is impressed.

One of the officers points to the clock. "Time for court."

A look of defeat crosses Dr. Peale's unshaven face. "Go. We have work to do here."

After the prisoner leaves, Dr. Peale fills in Franklin's back story for the new med students. "He was just a toddler sitting in his high chair when the shooting took place. He won't talk about it. He just doesn't want to deal with it."

The terms "teaching unit" and "therapeutic community" form a bitter taste in Carole's mouth. It appears to her that patients are just human specimens put in a fishbowl for training purposes. But, being the new kid on the block, she tucks her discontent in her back pocket. She suspects the psychiatrists might be worried less about patients and more that their impeccably footnoted therapeutic community is in serious disarray and that someone's going to ask why.

Dr. Schubachs asks, "Carole, you were right in the room when this happened. How do you feel about it?"

Carole just mumbles, "I hope Angela's OK."

For the remainder of group Carole's mind remains fixated on the term *statutory rape*. She plans to ask her therapist what that is, but in private.

As the meeting ends and Carole leaves the room, the unit nurse tells her, "Dr. Schubachs wants to see you in her office tomorrow at 1."

"Thanks," she mutters. "I've got lots to talk about."

# 9

At precisely noon the following day, Dr. Schubachs enters her office, kicks off her shoes and retrieves the bag lunch she brought from home. She fills her mug with the dregs from a coffee maker that's been brewing all morning, then settles down to check her phone messages as she eats.

"Can't find the damn car keys," Jake complains in one. "Thought you might know where I left them. Stupid of me to think I could reach you." His voice is punctuated with sarcasm as he slams the phone in its cradle.

Betty sighs, then moves on to the second call.

"Got the tickets you wanted," her mother reports. "Two front seats for *Do Patent Leather Shoes Really Reflect Up?* We'll enjoy it...especially with your convent experiences. You can use a little humor, Betty. Laughter is good medicine for what ails you. I prescribe a little more of it."

"Never stop your mothering, do you?" she chuckles out loud.

Next Schubachs transcribes admission notes for future reference while she nibbles on carrots and celery. The psychiatrist relies heavily on first impressions; they're key in her assignment. She ends with Carole. "Patient's appearance, behavior, and language all suggest sexual abuse is in the picture. Will explore this further." she concludes.

Schubachs shuts off the recorder to focus on her lunch in earnest. Eating at her desk isn't good for the digestion but it's become a habit of late, a sure sign of work overload. She gulps down the last bitter dregs, hoping the caffeine fix will get her through the rest of a long afternoon ahead.

Carole arrives at the door that reads Dr. Elizabeth Schubachs, M.D. shouldering a boatload of cynicism toward therapy relationships. They don't seem to work for her. She's seen them all: psychologists, psychiatrists, family therapists, priest counselors, and every other mental health position listed in the *Dictionary of Occupational Titles*.

She's attended, even led self-help groups like Recovery, Inc. where she faithfully followed methods outlined in Dr. Low's book, *Mental Health Through Will-Training*.

They all provided temporary relief, but the depression and suicidal urges habitually swell in intensity.

Carole looks around the psychiatrist's simple office: a desk, a file, two chairs, fluorescent lighting, and glass walls, designed to convey the image of transparency.

"So what do you think of group?" the therapist begins after her patient sits down.

"Too early to tell," she responds. "I prefer a wait-and-see approach."

"I've been going over your intake interview," Dr. Schubachs says. "My off-the-cuff diagnosis? You're not going to get better 'til you deal with the sexual abuse by your former therapists."

"A-abuse?" Carole stutters. "I never thought of it as *abuse*. No one ever suggested that's what it was."

She thought it was therapeutic at the time. Until she stopped trusting Dr. Jansen and she started to look for a way out of the relationship, not at all sure of what he was up to.

"How long did you see the doctor?"

"Too long. Until I could get strong enough to break away from him. I depended on him. Being thrown from the isolation of the convent into the turbulent '60's was tough. My nun therapist sent me to him for help in transitioning. The convent was an asexual world, far removed from the free sex prevalent in that decade."

"What did other therapists call it, if not abuse?" Dr. Schubachs inquires.

Carole stares at a cockroach attempting to escape the blinding light cast by fluorescent lights by burrowing itself under a waste basket in the corner of the room. "No one thought it important enough to talk about. I told all of them, just like I told you. No one ever brought it up again or asked me anything about it. So I thought it was unimportant."

"Look at me. Listen closely." Schubachs waits until Carole makes eye contact.

"It's the therapist's responsibility to control what happens in therapy. Having sex with a patient is never okay. It's unprofessional." She studies Carole's face for a reaction and finds none. "Having sex with a patient distracts both of you from the real problems you need to solve."

She pauses to let that message sink it, then continues. "And it causes *more* problems. It's malpractice at least, and possibly even statutory rape. Get it?"

Carole nods because that's what's expected of her, but what she carries back with her to the unit is a boatload of doubt and confusion. No one else suggested that dealing with what happened was the key to her healing. Why believe Schubachs? And how was she supposed to *deal with it*? She's resolved to do whatever it takes to get better, or die trying, so she'll find out what that entails.

In the seclusion of her private bathroom—one of the few places where Dr. Schubachs feels safe—the Betty in her explodes. "That son of a bitch!"

The intensity of her own anger surprises the psychiatrist. Carole's story reminds her of the sexual harassment she's had to face during her own medical training. She shakes her head in a futile attempt to destroy those painful memories. Anger surfaces at the most inopportune moment, just when she needs to maintain a professional composure.

"Me, too, Carole. Me, too," she mutters, then begins breathing exercises—the kind she recommends to patients zooming out of control. Gradually, the Hulk in her recedes. She turns to the mirror, straightens a strand of hair that has slipped out of place, and morphs back into Dr. Elizabeth Schubachs, M.D. Her next patient waits in the reception area.

# *10*

Once back in her bedroom, Carole loses herself in the shoals of her turbulent past. She flops on her bed, pulls a pillow over her head to block out the tempest, and exhausted, falls asleep.

Upon awakening, Carole confronts the Dr. Schubachs who threatens to take up residency in her psyche.

"Go away. There's no way you could understand what it was like back then. No way. Why should I even try to explain?"

Anger bubbles up like spitfire in a volcano about to erupt. She spews her fury in a journal entry for the day.

*You weren't isolated from the outside world during your teens—no radio, no magazines, no newspapers, no phone calls, no leaving campus to shop or to see a movie of your own choosing or just to enjoy a root beer float at an A & W with a friend.*

*In bed by 8:30 and up by 5:45, morning prayer by 6:15 then Mass. Love everyone, they taught us, but don't have best friends or you're out of here.*

*Did you have to ask permission for everything, even to go to the dorm to care for your personal hygiene at that special time of the month?*

*And then, after all of their myriad restrictions, I was suddenly out on my own in a world at war with itself.*

After taking a drink, Carole continues her rant.

*I'm from the Silent Generation. We carry the scars of WWII. We knew fear and scarcity. You didn't. You're a Baby Boomer, conceived in hope and security. I'll bet you grew up in some fancy suburban home. How else could you afford medical school?*

*Hey, Dr. Know-it-all, you were just a kid in the '60's! I lived it.*

She begins to document horrors of that violent decade that brought America to its knees.

*Bet you never saw city blocks burning. Or heard gunshots peppering the night while the National Guard, parked in your backyard, tried to contain the civil disorder. You didn't watch police violence directed at civilians during the Civil Rights marches—brought into your living room every night in vivid black and white.*

*You didn't grieve the assassinations of John F. Kennedy, Robert Kennedy, and Martin Luther King.*

*You didn't have friends, fellow Americans, flee to Canada to dodge a war they wanted no part of. You didn't cry out when guardsmen opened fire on student protesters at Kent University.*

*Did you sing "Blowin' in the Wind" with Peter, Paul and Mary? Of course not! You probably sang "Puff the Magic Dragon".*

*And you didn't hear church bells calling people to pray away the nuclear war fomenting off the coast of Florida, either.*

Carole pauses to reminisce before continuing her tirade.

*It was a time of revolutions.* Leave it to Beaver *disappeared when June Cleaver burned her bra and Masters and Johnson made sex the topic of public conversation. It was a different world with hippies, drugs, the flower children, Woodstock, and Stonewall.*

Even the remembering exhausts her, but she's not done yet. It was personal.

*I was drowning—alone in a cesspool of cultural and personal discontent. I needed something, someone to hang on to. Because I trusted the nun therapist who referred me to Dr. Jansen, I trusted him. I shouldn't have.*

Caught up in a cacophony of defensiveness and self-blame, Carole blocks out Dr. Schubachs' message of support, not blame. Finally it begins to siphon through the muck.

*Could it have been his fault?* Carole wonders. Her rant evolves into a plan of action.

*I don't have to trust you, Dr. Schubachs. I can research this at the university library. I can find out what other experts say. All I need from you is a pass to get there.*

Carole shakes her head to banish the phantom therapist. But it's too late. Dr. Schubachs has already burrowed her way deep into Carole's psyche, and she's not leaving soon.

A journey of discovery begins. The journey backwards moves Carole forward.

# 11

In sports there is the timeout; in careers, a sabbatical or leave of absence; in the spiritual realm, a retreat. In all of these, a person pauses to review the past, to examine the present, and to plan for the future. Carole's time in the mental health center could be likened to these. She takes a much needed break from husband and three small children to insure a better future for them, one that isn't tarnished by her past.

In the next few months Carole will crisscross the time zones of her life tooled with introspection, reverie, investigation, and therapy in her search for a much desired cure. Eventually, she hopes a new, healthier woman will emerge. As part of this process, she recalls childhood influences still at play in her adult life.

When in the mindset of her younger self, Carole records memories of her youth . . .

*I always see a crucifix above my teacher's desk, next to the American flag . . . Jesus stares down at me, bloody tears on his face, and a crown of prickly thorns on his head. Sometimes I prick myself on a rose bush to see what that might feel like.*

*I see a statue of the Blessed Mother Mary in every classroom. Girls are supposed to be like the Virgin Mary. I have no idea what a virgin is. I pray the Rosary, "Hail Mary: give us world peace and bless the pagan babies." The Rosary is real boring though; we say the same Hail Mary fifty-three times. But I do it 'cuz I like Mary. She has such a pretty smile. I don't like the snake she stands on though. That's creepy!*

*I hear someone use the word "mantra". I ask my mother what that means. She says ask your father, he's smarter. He tells me a mantra is a word repeated over and over and over again. Like the Hail Mary, I think.*

*I ask Dad if "Sister says" could be a mantra, too. I hear that at school all the time.*

*"Not really," he says hardly glancing up from the sports section.*

*In my school you better do what Sister says. I love my teachers even though they dress funny. I wish I could see their hair but it's all tucked under their veils. Sometimes a piece slips out. I saw Sister Monica turn away to push it back in once. I think she has black hair but I'm not sure. I wonder if nuns ever eat or go to the bathroom.*

*My big sister got sent home for wearing a bare midriff blouse to her class picnic. Sister Grace scolded her right in front of everyone. "The least you could do is wear a dress that meets in the middle!" she said.*

*My sister didn't see anything wrong with showing her tummy at a picnic, but in my school whatever SISTER SAYS goes, so she came home and changed.*

*I wanna be a nun. I plan to enter the convent just as soon as I can. I practice putting a towel around my head in front of the mirror.*

*Or else I'll marry an Indian. I read lots of books about them. I've read about Sitting Bull, Crazy Horse, and Chief Joseph. They took good care of their people and were very brave when things got tough. Chief Joseph is my very favorite. He was smart, smarter than the cavalry. They couldn't catch him for the longest time. I want to be brave and smart like him.*

*Sometimes I pretend I am an Indian girl. I put my doll in a cradleboard my father made for me. I read* Indian Captive *by Lois Lenski. I wish I'd be adopted into an Indian tribe like Mary Jemison was. I see a picture of her gathering corn. She has no top on, just leggings and a buckskin skirt. I like her cuz she has tiny breasts popping out. Mine are starting to do that, too. No one makes fun of her for that. It's just the way bodies are in Indian times.*

*Sometimes I'm as quiet as a mouse so I can hear Mom and Dad talking when they don't know I'm listening. Today I heard Dad talking about something called POOBER TEA. I don't know what that is. He thinks I've caught it. How do you catch tea? I don't know why he thinks that. I don't feel sick or anything. Mom disagrees. She says I'm way too young for that. I figure it must be something you get when you're older. I'm only eight going on nine. I guess Mom ought to know. She's a nurse; he's just a chemist who changes the color of water. What could he know about POOBER TEA?*

*I hear him laugh in a funny kind of way. "I think you're wrong, Rose. Don't say I didn't warn you."*

*Sister says Eve caused all the evil in the world. Eve is a Bible lady who runs around buck naked. She is bad—very bad, the baddest person in the whole human race. Being naked is a lot worse than wearing a bare midriff!*

*Eve should never have talked to that snake. He coaxed her into eating an apple from the forbidden tree. Then she turned around and gave one to Adam.*

*Father Sinclair says Adam just did what she told him to do, so it was really Eve's fault we got in trouble. Thanks to her we all got stained with Original Sin. I wonder what Original Sin looks like anyway. Is it like mud on your soul? Can Holy Water wash it away? Maybe it's like the snake the Virgin Mary crushes under her feet?*

*That's kind of why I don't like being a girl that much. Girls are pretty screwed-up because of Eve. My parents think boys are much more special. So does my big brother. He says he doesn't have to do dishes, not with three sisters to do them. He has a paper route instead. And money to spend. I want to be like him. It bothers me that he is special and I am not.*

The adult Carole feels sorry for that little girl whose body matured too early for her mind to understand what was happening. Sad, she thinks, that no one took time to help her understand. She likes this little girl who thinks deep thoughts and dreams big dreams.

What happened to that little girl anyway?

# 12

"In the convent I was taught, 'Don't depend on other people; don't get attached'," she told Dr. Schubachs. "I didn't listen. I let myself get dependent on my therapist. Then I couldn't get away from him," she explained to her new therapist. "My bad."

"Not so," said Dr. Schubachs. "It was his."

Out of curiosity, Carole checks the yellow pages to see if he still practices in the area. His name is there, under 'psychiatrists.' Harry Jansen, M.D. Same address, same phone number . . . just a few miles down the road . . . in the same building . . . doing the same thing, she wonders.

"It's been a long time since I mustered enough courage to walk out of that office for good. He's gotta be much older, but wiser? Probably not."

In an office across town, Dr. Harry Jansen sits in his recliner, sipping whiskey. He hears the waiting room door open and shut and checks his afternoon schedule. Must be Sharon Scranton's client, one of her referrals from the Department of Vocational Rehabilitation.

The two of them connected at a local pub months ago. Sharon was pissed at her old man, Jansen listened, the two connected, and ended up in the sack afterwards. They've been drinking buddies and more ever since. Jansen considers the relationship a win-win for both of them.

The physician places his glass in the lamp stand, then scribbles a note to self on the palm of his hand. *Stop at the liquor store.*

It's getting harder to remember things of late. Foggy brain syndrome, his ex calls it. Dan the Man compensates by scribbling notes on his unusually large hand. He's got to remember to check it. This very morning he forgot an appointment. When he retrieved a call from an impatient patient, he scurried to his office but didn't make it in time. The man was gone, along with his hourly fee.

Jansen slips on his loafers and pulls his lanky figure out of the recliner. He puts a sports coat on over his turtleneck sweater, then buttons up his sans-a-belt slacks before opening the door that leads to the reception area.

The psychiatrist drapes his arm around the young man's shoulder as he guides his new patient in. Not a good move. The man detects a smell of whiskey on the therapist's breath and squirms loose.

The interview is routine. Short personal history. Psychological issues. Current retraining goals. The psychiatrist stifles a yawn. All this client needs is the physician's signature on the governmental form, and a follow-up written recommendation on letterhead stationery.

"If you have any questions, Sharon says you should call her," the patient reports, handing over the familiar form.

The psychiatrist searches for a working pen, finds one under some loosely scattered papers. After playing a version of Russian Roulette with DSM-III labels, he selects an appropriate one. Patient needs a label to get services, but he can't be so sick that retraining would be a waste of tax payers' money. Jansen enters a diagnosis, scrawls his signature on the form, He then slips it into an envelope, seals it and hands it back.

"Give this to your counselor. Good luck."

After showing the patient out, the psychiatrist eases back into his recliner, retrieves his carefully concealed glass. The place is way too quiet. Jack Daniels has become his best companion of late.

When opening his practice Jansen decided to go on his own. He didn't need any office personnel snooping around. As a pediatrician, he learned that oversight creates problems. A concerned secretary reported his drinking to management. The internal investigation landed him in an impaired physician program, and eventually cost him his job.

"Why is it I can cure other people's children but I can do nothing to stop my own little girl's deteriorating condition?" Jansen complained to his alcohol counselor. "I feel so impotent."

"Consider retraining in another field," his counselor advised." Get away from pediatrics, where you'll be reminded every day of your daughter's limitations and your inability to cure her."

Jansen did just that. He chose psychiatry, knowing he could have his own private practice with no one looking over his shoulder. After finishing a year of residency at the VA hospital, he set up his own practice. That was fifteen years ago, about the time the nun referred Carole to him.

Jansen reaches for the phone, dials Sharon's number. "Wanna meet at the pub tonight? You can help me with that letter for your client."

That, they both understand, is code for something much more intimate.

# 13

Back at the Mental Health Center Carole continues to journal in her childhood persona, still searching for insight into what ails her.

*It's 1947. I visit Grandma sometimes. Mom hates her. Their fighting scares me. My brother and sisters are on Mom's side. I'm not.*

*I don't like Grandma that much but she is Dad's mom. He wants someone to like her. I try to, for his sake. I visit her when he goes over to play cards but I won't stay overnight.*

*I notice Grandma has a red satin pillow with gold braid fringes on it. She says my uncle sent it to her from the South Pacific where he's stationed. I memorize the words embroidered on it. "There is so much good in the worst of us and so much bad in the best of us that it never behooves any of us to talk about the rest of us." Next to it I see the name "Abraham Lincoln."*

*I know who Lincoln is. I heard about the Civil War in school. Sometimes I feel like there is a civil war going on right in our house. I'm tired of dodging the bullets. I hate to hear the telephone ring. It might be Grandma firing a warning shot—another battle's coming. I hate to see my mother cry, and she always cries when the fight is over.*

*I get what Lincoln is saying. We aren't all good or all bad. There are some good things about Grandma. I think she is a good cook, even though Mom says she isn't. Grandma always has a pretty Christmas tree. She gives us money for Christmas and I like that. I get to drink Canada Dry ginger ale and eat Geyser's potato chips at her house.*

*I don't get it why she keeps Grandpa in the basement except at meal time. That just doesn't seem fair. I ask Dad why she does that. He mutters something about a Catholic divorce but he says I am too young to understand. I guess I don't. Grandpa seems like a nice man to me.*

*Lincoln wrote we shouldn't spread bad things about each other. Especially things that start fights, I think. I promise myself that I will never repeat the mean things Grandma says that might upset my mother. My brother and sisters do that all the time. Don't they get it? It's like putting coal in our basement furnace. Someone could get burnt!*

*I may be young but what I do know is that a war going on in your own home is the worst kind of war. It's hard to get away from it.*

Carole has kept quiet about Dr. Jansen just like she learned to keep quiet about Grandma. Maybe it's time to rethink that. *What if he's hurting someone else? Maybe I shouldn't keep quiet about what he did. Maybe I should stop protecting Dr. Jansen.*

Carole upsets her therapist during their next therapy session. "I've been thinking a lot about what you said last time." She weighs her words carefully. "No offense, but I'm not sure I believe what you said last time—about that *abuse* stuff. Why didn't other therapists ever tell me this was abuse?"

Dr. Schubachs bristles at this challenge to her authority. "What he did was abuse. Plain and simple."

Reading her therapist's angry body language, Carole backs away, allows her to set the agenda.

"I gave you a job to do," Schubachs says. "Did you give any thought to how he groomed you?"

"A little. If you mean he did it in steps. I guess that might describe what happened. I just never thought of it as grooming."

"Sexual predators are clever and extremely skillful at manipulation," the psychiatrist opines.

"I guess. I do see a pattern in what he did. When he prescribed birth control pills, it wasn't really to counteract my acne at all. He must have had something else in mind!"

"You're right, Carole. Why would he choose birth control pills to combat your acne when there are other products that can do that?"

Out of a deeply engrained habit Carole jumps to Dr. Jansen's defense. "He did it for my own good. Don't you get it? I was terrified of my own body. God made me a sexual being. He wouldn't want me to be afraid of my own body."

"What do you mean? Jansen helped you? I don't think so."

"At least he didn't bury his head in the sand. My Mom told me nothing about sex. When she caught my brother and me and some neighborhood kids playing doctor, she sent my friends away. She said I couldn't play with them anymore. Who was I suppose to play with? Losing friends is a big thing to a little girl who's shy. She didn't send my brother's friends away. Just mine."

"No explanation?"

"None."

"So when I started to bleed, I thought God was punishing me, just like she did. She never warned me that was going to happen." Carole's face turns bright red as she reports, "I was only nine and so ashamed when the back of my dress was blood-stained. I was sure everyone could see what was happening to me."

"I guess she really missed the boat on that one," Dr. Schubachs comments.

Carole continues to relate a scanty sex education. "When I was a senior in high school, a priest explained to the class how babies were made. Afterwards he told us to take a shower, like we were dirty from the telling."

"When I asked my college biology teacher a question about sex, the nun called me a boor. I went to the unabridged dictionary to find out what that meant. *Boor: a person with rude, clumsy manners.* That really hurt! It was the one and only time I dared to talk to anyone about sex."

"Sounds to me like a teacher who wasn't comfortable talking about sex so she said that to shut you up," Dr. Schubachs suggests. "It worked, didn't it?"

"Guess so."

There's a long pause before Carole finally breaks the silence. "At least Dr. Jansen tried to help me."

"You're still defending him, Carole. Why? He didn't HELP you." She leans forward to emphasize her point. "Look at you now. Are you better? Are you happy? Do you have a healthy sex life?"

"Stop! Stop this." Carole puts her hands over her ears. "I don't even know who I am anymore. I don't know what's wrong! Or who's wrong! How do I know *you're* right? Why should I trust *you* anymore than all the other therapists?"

The psychiatrist pulls back and steers the rest of their time to less threatening topics: Carole's adaptation to the unit, family visits, off-unit activities. As Carole gets up to leave, Dr. Schubachs poses a parting challenge: "Do you think you'll ever do something about the therapists who abused you?"

The patient has a plan in mind but she's not ready to share it with her therapist yet. Instead she requests a pass to go to campus, explaining she needs to meet with her advisor to schedule classes for next semester.

"I think you're ready for a pass. I'll write it for next Thursday."

Carole leaves, puzzled over her therapist's suggestion that she do something.

"What am I supposed to do?" Carole mutters as she strolls back to her unit. "I'm just a psych patient—an hysterical woman according to my last doctor . . ."

# 14

Dawn Dailey, department chair and graduate student advisor, takes her role seriously. People in advanced study are frequently making significant life changes. She aims to provide support and guidance in that process. In her introductory class, she requires new students to submit three papers up front: one that describes a childhood fantasy of what life would be all about; one that describes the student's current status; and one that describes the person's expectations for the future. She uses these assignments to build a solid mentor relationship with each student.

In the 1980's, the professor sees many women like Carole who are restless and dissatisfied with a traditionally-assigned homemaker role. She often steers them towards women's studies as an elective. As an admitted feminist, Dawn believes consciousness-raising in this era of shifting gender expectations is a gift one woman gives to another.

The professor learned of Carole's emotional struggles early on when the student excused herself halfway through her very first class, explaining she needed to check in at the emergency room a few blocks away.

When Dawn called later to inquire about Carole's condition, she was surprised when the student's number connected her to a nearby psychiatric hospital ward. Carole apologized for leaving, explaining she had consumed a whole bottle of Tylenol on the way to class, then thought better of what she had done.

She reported that after pumping her stomach to prevent permanent liver damage, an angry emergency room doctor scolded her.

"I'm okay now. Just a bit of foolishness on my part."

Dawn believes concern, not anger, is a more humane treatment, and a far better way to assuage Carole's despair.

From that point on she focuses on building Carole's confidence in her own ability to transition from full-time homemaker to a career woman. How best to serve women like her is the topic of many campus discussions. *Displaced homemakers* is the current nomenclature.

When a colleague charged with developing a new Women's Career Center requests a graduate student to do library research on women's career paths, Dawn suggests Carole. Such research might contribute to her mentee's own personal growth, she reasons. Today's meeting is to update the professor on how the research project is going, and to complete registration for the next semester's coursework.

"Come on in, Carole," Dawn invites, looking up from a desk cluttered with student papers, family photos, and freshly-cut daffodils. "Sit, sit." She gestures to a chair adjacent to her desk. "How are you doing?" she begins.

"I guess I'm doing okay. Were you surprised when I told you I was out at County now?"

"Not really," Dawn replies. "I know things are touch and go with you now."

"I have a woman therapist this time."

"A female therapist might be just what you need," Dawn nods. "How about a cup of tea?" she suggests.

"Sure."

Dawn moves across the room to where she keeps a hot pot going for times like this. She fixes a cup of herbal tea, and hands it to Carole, asking how the research project is going.

Carole opens her brief case and pulls out a document. "Here's a rough draft of my report for the Women's Center. I brought a copy. I'd love your feedback before I submit it."

Dawn sets the paper aside, promising to read it later.

"While you're here, how about registering for next semester?" her advisor suggests.

"Preregistration time already. How quickly time is moving along. I want to do independent study if that's an option."

Dawn has a different option in mind: community placement. Graduate students not currently working in the field of study profit from internships. She shares information about a six week training program about to begin at the Women's Crisis Line. It provides training and on-the-job experience for volunteers who answer crisis calls.

The advisor explains that the Women's Crisis Line provides the most comprehensive training on women's issues in the city. Professionals provide training in their own areas of expertise in intensive workshops that last all day for six Saturdays. Newly trained volunteers are then matched with those experienced in handling calls.

"Can you manage that?" Dawn asks.

"These are all very current topics," Carole observes as she studies the curriculum. "Sexual abuse, rape, domestic violence, marital property, displaced homemakers…A chance to help other women. That's cool. Can I apply?"

"I'll write a referral and do the paperwork the university requires for awarding credit. You get the pass to go. I assume you'll need that from your therapist."

The phone interrupts their conversation. Dawn answers and puts the caller on hold. "Gotta take this, sorry," she says. "A problem at home needs attention. I think we're about finished anyway."

Carole gets up to leave.

"So how do you plan to spend rest of your day?" Dawn asks, as she escorts Carole out the door.

"Oh, I've got research to do in the library," Carole mutters, not getting into specifics.

"If I can help in any way, call," her adviser says, as she closes the door.

Carole has many questions whirling in her head. But there's one that no amount of library research will answer: *Is Dr. Jansen still having sex with other patients?*

# *15*

5:15 P.M. The door to the outer office opens and shuts. Must be the twenty-year-old girl who's been coming at her parents' insistence, Dr. Jansen surmises.

The psychiatrist reflects on this case. Mom and Dad are totally at a loss on what to do with their daughter, who shows no interest in dating. She'll never find Mr. Right, they fear. They believe that's what college is for. This one is not like her sisters. She navigates toward women, not men. Mom choked on the L word as she labeled her daughter's problem.

The young woman's conservative parents believe such perversion is a Biblical abomination. Ashamed to share their dilemma with friends or family, desperate to find a cure, they are seeking professional help for her, and are willing to pay for it.

The doctor has a cure in mind, his own brand of *conversion therapy*, much gentler than what colleagues are using these days. It's common practice to use progressively intense electroshock or nausea-inducing drugs or even chemical castration to purge same-sex tendencies. Jansen's got a better method. Pleasure not pain is the basis of his reparative therapy.

Jansen adjusts his boxer shorts, grown uncomfortably tight as he contemplates the evening session. He scheduled Marjorie last. He needs time and privacy to administer his treatment.

*I need a drink to set the mood. Maybe she does, too. Hmm…Scotch might loosen her up.* He reaches in his stand, pulls out two glasses. He then selects romantic music and tones down the lights, before opening the door to the inner office.

"Come on in, Marjorie," he says, as he escorts her into his lair.

Dr. Jansen curses as he slams the door after Marjorie leaves. "Stubborn bitch pushed me away!" he grumbles, frustrated by his patient's sound rejection of his advances.

The phone rings as he readies to leave for home. Twelve-year-old daughter Lucy. All the problems of the day fade away when he hears his little girl's voice.

*Oh, Lucy, we named you well. You bring light into my world like no one else can. You make this troublesome job worthwhile.*

"What are you doing still up at this hour of the night?" he asks.

"Daddy, I miss you. Are you coming over soon?" a tiny voice whines. "I'm hungry."

"I'll be there soon," he assures his little sweetheart.

On the way, Jansen picks up a cheese and sausage frozen pizza, Lucy's favorite. She's up in her wheelchair waiting in the kitchen when he pulls into the driveway. He sees her peeking out the window.

Maxine, Lucy's live-in nurse, greets Jansen at the side door. "It's your ex's monthly night out with the girls," she says. "She'll be late. Lucy insists on waiting up for you. I hope you don't mind."

"Are you kidding?" Jansen assures Max. "Not at all. She's the sunshine of my life. Lucy said she was hungry. Can I get you to bake this?"

He hands the pizza to Maxine, hugs Lucy and wheels his daughter into the living room. "Tell me about your day, Lucy."

Yelping sounds fill the room as Lucy demonstrates how her new Cocker Spaniel puppy just learned to beg. The little guy strains mightily to control his puppy energy. At Lucy's command he sits on his haunches, almost, then springs prematurely for the doggy treat in Lucy's hands. She rewards him with a hug and buries her face in his fur. That brings a smile to Harry's face.

# 16

Carole is so deeply engrossed in research she loses track of time and almost misses her bus back to the County. She scurries directly to Dr. Schubachs' office for her scheduled appointment. Both arrive at the same time, Carole a bit out of breath, the therapist calm and cool as always. The therapy room floods with light as they enter.

"Just came from the University," she says as soon as she catches her breath. "I've got loads to share. I spent the afternoon researching client-therapist sex. There's tons of info out there."

"So, what did you learn?" her therapist asks as she takes a seat opposite her patient.

"Loads. The Hippocratic Oath specifically warns physicians 'to abstain from the seduction of females or males.' The same admonition appears in most professional ethics codes."

Schubachs is confident in her own perspective but assumes the role of devil's advocate to test her patient's insight. "The Hippocratic Oath . . . hmm, that's from ancient Greece, not the twentieth century. And we're not in the Victorian Age either. We're post-1960. Sex is a part of life so what's the big deal?" the therapist wheedles.

"It is a big deal or I wouldn't have found so much written about it," Carole responds irritably. "Did you know 7 to 10% of therapists admit to having sex with a client? It's a big deal when they ruin people's lives!"

"Therapy is an intimate relationship," Schubachs comments, egging her on. "Not surprising it could lead to sex."

Carole's face turns read with anger. "Don't minimize this. Broken vows . . . unwanted pregnancies . . . moral confusion. Patients walk out of the office with more problems than they carried in!"

"You've got a point," Schubachs responds. "And the problems they came to solve never get addressed."

Carole's voice grows louder and louder. "The therapist is *always* the one in control. Therapy is never a level playing field." She glares at Dr. Schubachs. "You guys know all our secrets, all our weaknesses; we don't know yours. I haven't a clue what's going on in your life."

The therapist is pleased to see her patient's new understanding growing but the intensity of her anger is a bit alarming. When Carole gets out of her seat and begins pacing, the therapist places her hand on the hidden panic button—just in case the session gets out of hand. "So tell me about all the power I have," she says, goading her patient on.

"You prescribe drugs to control us. You diagnose us, label us, create medical records that follow us for a lifetime. You get paid for your expertise, even when you're dead wrong. You testify in court, and people believe you, cuz you're the *expert*. You lock us up and dole out 'privileges' at your whim." Carole moves closer taking on an in-your-face stance. "The night I arrived here, you took away my clothes and everything I brought along. You allowed an invasive body search, put me through a supervised shower like I was a dirty piece of shit! I took a shower that morning, just like you did."

It's starting to get a little too personal. Dr. Schubachs snaps back at her patient. "You can leave anytime you want!"

"Not everyone can," Carole retorts. "Some people have been put here by the court or by family members."

"You've made your point, Carole. Now, sit down."

The patient does as she's told. Her breathing subsides as her adrenaline dissipates. Eventually, in a more subdued, almost sad tone, she concludes, "I never found a single article that suggested how people might recover from a therapist's abuse."

An eerie silence follows. The only sound in the room is the relentless ticking of the wall clock. The office goes dark as the sensor fails to detect any motion.

When Dr. Schubachs shifts her position, the light flashes back on. "How did your meeting with your advisor go?" she asks.

Carole's demeanor changes. She's excited about the Women's Crisis Line training. She outlines what it's all about. She plans to apply.

"Great," Dr. Schubachs comments. "When you listen to the callers, I think you'll hear an echo of your own concerns."

"I like my advisor," Carole says. "She's a feminist. Just like you."

Taken aback, the doctor responds, "Me? What makes you think that?"

"The patients on your case load. Me—sexual abuse. The anorexic woman. The mom with postpartum depression. Aren't those pretty much women's issues?"

"It's nothing to do with my being a *feminist*," Schubachs reacts, irritated at being labeled. "We admit more women than men. That's why there are so many females on my caseload."

Carole neutralizes the tension in the room by detailing the contents of the upcoming training. The first session will be presented by two speakers, a woman from the Sensitive Crimes Unit of the District Attorney's office will discuss sexual assault, and an attorney who was previously employed in the same unit but now practices with a private law firm will discuss incest.

Dr. Schubachs scrawls something in Carole's chart while she listens. "I'm writing an order that allows you to attend the training."

"Thanks."

Dr. Schubachs leans against the door after Carole exits the office. She wasn't all together transparent with her patient. She had many feminist friends and allies at Mercy Hospital. And she misses them.

# 17

Back on the unit, Carole retreats into her past again. She begins to journal about the first time she shared her Dr. Jansen experience—with her family doctor.

*It was 1969. I was about to get married. According to the law I had to have an internal exam to get a marriage license. Since this was the first internal exam I ever had, I didn't know what to expect. I feared my family doctor would discover I wasn't a virgin, so I explained I had sex with a psychiatrist I had been seeing for therapy. His only comment was, "That man did you a great disservice."*

*In 1978 I brought Jake in for a healthy baby exam. My longtime GP paid more attention to me than Jake. I'd lost 75 pounds and couldn't explain why. He said something that made no sense to me. "You are being utterly consumed with rage."*

*I didn't get it. I didn't feel angry, just very, very depressed. I left, wondering what he meant.*

Totally exhausted from the day's events, Carole puts aside her journal and drifts off to sleep. In her dream she encounters her GP with the Teddy Bear brown eyes. Light pounces off his bald head just like it did when she was in his examining room as a child. He seems visibly upset with her.

"Why so mad at *me*?" she asks. "You were president of the County Medical Society. You could have done something but you didn't."

No response on the specter's part.

Carole wakes up with a start. "That's it. I'll file a complaint with the Medical Society."

Two days later Carole spots an obituary in the newspaper. Her family physician passed away the very night she dreamed about him. She speculates maybe he had some unfinished business to attend to before passing from this world to the next. Such are the mysteries of life and death that we know so little about.

Affirmed by the dream, she pursues in writing a formal complaint with the local Medical Society.

# 18

Like many grass roots organizations, the Women's Crisis Line is located in a marginal part of town. Carole checks out the street before leaving her car to walk to the old run down brick building in the outer rim of what was once a vibrant downtown neighborhood.

She arrives at the Center about the same time as a young woman, who introduces herself as Sally. Carole's apprehension diminishes as they engage in small talk.

"Ever hear Leanne speak? That's her." Sally points out the dark-haired thirty-something woman conversing with a handsome man in a business suit.

"You know Leanne?"

"Not really. Just heard her talk once. She's a social worker connected with the DA's office. She helps people who have to testify as witnesses in sensitive crime cases—sexual assault, domestic violence, incest, you know. She's just perfect for the job."

Carole reserves judgment for the time being. She deliberately chooses a front row seat where she can study the speaker's body language. By the time the clock strikes nine, twenty seats have filled in.

Leanne begins promptly. "Morning, everyone. Hope you've had a cup of coffee. You're gonna need the caffeine. We've got lots to cover today."

The chatter subdues as the audience shifts to attention.

"Kathy wants me to explain the work we do. She also wants me to teach you some techniques for handling crisis calls about sexual abuse—all in three hours time. Think we can do it?"

The trainees glance at each other, but no one chooses to respond.

"Come on folks. A little more life, please. If you need a waker-upper, there's a pot of coffee in the back of the room." She takes a sip from her own cup. "Black and strong, I guarantee."

A handful straggle to the back to get a caffeine fix. When all are back in place, Leanne begins.

She explains how the Sensitive Crimes Unit was created to support victims of sexual assault, incest, child abuse, and domestic violence in multiple ways.

"We support victims in their recovery, prepare them as witnesses, and accompany them to the courtroom when they testify. I'm here to talk specifically about sexual assault."

She pauses, shifts from a formal to a counselor's voice. "It's tough to talk about something as personal as sexual assault in a courtroom full of strangers."

Carole wonders if she would ever be able to do that. She finds herself drawn to this woman. Maybe with Leanne's help?

"Filing a complaint ain't easy. And it's never smooth sailing. Bad things can happen along the way. Can you think of hurdles that might arise?" she challenges.

Trainees call out possibilities. Loss of privacy . . . physical threats from the perpetrator . . . loss of a job . . . the possibility of a defamation suit . . . negative peer judgment . . . being seen as damaged goods by men she dates . . .

"Hey, give us some slack there," a male voice pops up. "That's not the way all men think."

"That's Jonathon, my friend and former colleague at the DA's office," Leanne interjects. "Guess we struck a nerve there, Jonathon. Sorry."

"Thought I give you a male perspective. I've been there. A person I loved was assaulted. Want to know how that feels? I'd like to rip that guy apart for what he did, and I can't." His voice falters. "There's always that elephant in the room keeping us apart and she won't even talk about it." A long pause while he tries to control his emotions.

"It was my fault for letting her go home alone but she insisted. I don't know what to do now, or what to say. So I stay away." Another pause. "Things just aren't the same between us."

"Well, folks, this is your first crisis call. How you gonna handle it?"

Any sleepyheads in the room are now fully alert, but too shy to answer.

Sally is first to speak up. "Where would you begin?"

"I'd listen." Leanne responds. "Did you? What did you hear in that man's voice? What's he feeling right now?"

Trainees call out: "Rage . . . helplessness . . . guilt . . . confusion . . . frustration . . . loneliness . . . sorrow . . . regret . . ."

"Great responses! Guess you're more awake than you appear." Nervous laughter breaks the tension in the room.

"Were you surprised that the call came from a friend not the victim herself?" Leanne says. "Often it's a friend or family member who is first to reach out for help."

"Seems like he's kind of a victim, too," Sally observes.

"He is. There's always more than one victim in a crime."

"One thing I heard—he wants to make things right again," Carole offers.

"Exactly. While he'd like to beat the shit out of the guy, he knows better. So he's looking for a better way to fix things. That's where you come in—with options we'll discuss in a minute."

"He needs to know that what happened is not his fault," Carole suggests.

"Good point. He is blaming himself, isn't he?"

"Kathy," Leanne calls out to the Crisis Line Counselor who co-ordinates the training. "Can you role play victim calling in?"

While waiting for Kathy to come to the front of the room, Leanne clarifies, "A common defense in rape cases is to argue the sex was consensual. Or that the victim asked for it. Her dress, language, behavior, sexual history, and credibility are all put to the test."

With Kathy now ready to play the part, the mock call begins. "Hi, um . . . I'm calling cuz my boyfriend said I should. He won't get off my back." Pause. "It's over and done with. Why won't he just let me forget?"

"Gotta tell you, I'm really proud of you for making this call," Leanne responds. "I know it isn't easy."

"Right," Kathy says. "I keep telling him I don't want to talk about what happened."

"Too painful, maybe?" Leanne suggests.

"I'm not a sissy," Kathy insists. "I don't cry over spilled milk. I'm a big girl now."

"No, you're not a sissy!" Leanne assures her. "Not at all. Something really bad happened to you."

"Yeah but it was my own fault," Kathy confesses. "I was so stupid!"

"Why do you say that?" Leanne asks.

"I dressed up real sexy that night," Kathy begins. "My best dress, perfume, heels. The works. Even had my hair done. I planned a special night for the two of us."

"Nice. I can relate to that," Leanne says. "Don't we all love to put our best foot forward for that special someone?"

"Then the two of us got into a fight over something stupid," Kathy recalls. "I can't even remember what it was about. I was so mad I stalked out of the bar. Told him I'd find my own way home."

"Lover's quarrels can be a real bitch," Leanne agrees.

"I started walking. After four blocks. I took off my shoes. My feet were killing me. Then I picked up the pace. At one point, I stopped to rest on a bench. A really nice guy came by and asked if I needed a ride home. At least I thought he was nice."

Kathy stops to blow her nose. "I know I shouldn't have said yes, but my feet where killing me, so I climbed into his car. Gave him my address. When he drove right past my place, I knew I was in trouble. I tried getting out when he parked but he came after me so fast. He was so strong…"

"That must have been very frightening," Leanne suggests.

"It was all my fault, I was so stupid," Kathy mumbles.

"Good job, Kathy. We'll stop here. I need to get moving along or we'll never cover everything."

The social worker continues with her prepared material. "Victims obsess about what they did wrong," Leanne elaborates. "The truth is they did nothing to merit what happened to them. We need to assure women, and men too, that when they say no and are forced into sexual acts, that's rape."

A question comes from the back of the room. "Should we encourage victims to contact you? If so, how soon should they do so?"

"As soon as they are ready to do so. As soon as possible, while evidence is still fresh."

"Not everyone will choose to testify," Jonathon pipes up. "Not every case will end up in the courtroom."

"But every victim can use help," Leanne responds. "We'll do what we can to help, even if all we do is listen."

"What if a person decides to press charges?" Sally asks. "And they lose in court? That'd really hurt."

"We always discuss that possibility," Leanne says. "If a jury determines there's not enough evidence to convict, it doesn't mean the rape never occurred."

"If that happens, it must feel like no one believes her or no one cares," Sally complains.

"That's why we don't rush into court with just any case."

Sally asks, this time more haltingly, "What if the person can't testify? What if they just aren't . . . strong enough?"

"Old cases are harder to prosecute. The statute of limitations can be an insurmountable barrier."

"So if it happened a long time ago, should they even bother to contact you?" Carole asks.

A sad look passes over Leanne's face. "I'm willing to talk to any victim, but it's unlikely charges can be filed."

Carole stares at the floor. Crap! A dead end. Her time for doing anything is long gone.

"I can tell by the look on your face that doesn't make you happy. Me either. We're working with the legislature to change that."

Carole's moment passes.

"One last caution: don't make decisions for your callers," Leanne warns. "Suggest options, but let them choose their course of action. Victims need to regain a sense of control, something they lost in the rape."

For the last fifteen minutes the trainees simulate calls with one another. Carole surmises from comments she hears that the room is full of wounded healers. Makes sense. It's give-back time for them, and part of their recovery.

Finally Kathy announces, "Times up. There's coffee, soda, sandwiches, bakery. Picnic bench is in the yard. Get a bit of fresh air, if you want, or eat at the kitchen table in back. Be back in forty-five minutes."

# 19

When the trainees reassemble, Kathy formally introduces the next speaker: Attorney Jonathon Prospect, once employed in the Sensitive Crimes Unit, recently hired by the prestigious law office of Jones, Smythe, and Crawford. "Jonathon will talk about incest, a special kind of sexual assault. It's messy, extremely complicated. You'll soon see what I mean."

Kathy hands the mike to Jonathon, then pulls it back momentarily to clarify a point of concern that came up during the break. "Our language sucks, folks! I wish we had a gender-neutral term to use in our discussions. We don't. All the *he* and *she* . . . we know males can be victims and females can be perpetrators. This being the *Women's* Crisis Line, we fall into the habit of saying she for victims and he for perpetrators 'cause we don't get many calls from male victims. We know they're out there. Maybe someday they'll find a way to communicate their pain, too."

"Thanks for clarifying that, Kathy," Jonathan smiles, adjusting the mike for his greater height. Paradoxically, while his mannerisms are informal, casual, and friendly, his attorney's demeanor exudes confidence and authority.

He turns to Leanne, his former colleague and now friend. "Feel free to jump in whenever you have something to add. I know my way around the courtroom better than the therapy office."

He clears his throat, adjust his notes on the podium, and begins. "I asked a certain brave young lady to share what she told me during the break. Mary, please." He hands one of the trainees the mic.

"I told Jonathon I have a cousin Joanie whose father, eh, abused her," Mary begins, softly, tenuously. "Umm . . . My aunt was furious when Joanie reported her dad to a school counselor. He denied it."

She takes on a sheepish look. "We believed him instead of Joanie. When the facts finally came out, it turned out it really happened. With all the publicity, he lost his job. Without his income, things got rough for them. The family blamed Joanie, called her liar at first, then a tattler. My cousins even ended up in foster care for awhile."

When Mary finds it hard to continue, Jonathan steps in momentarily, reassuring her. "The loss of a breadwinner is no small thing. I've seen it happen. That's hard on everyone."

Mary gets a grip, enough to continue. "What a family upheaval! My uncle was always really a nice guy. That's why we found it hard to believe. When I saw Joanie cutting herself, I just thought she was weird and I stayed as far away from her as I could. Eventually she ran away. Wish I knew then what I know now. I could have been more of a support."

"Thanks for sharing, Mary. I know that wasn't easy."

"Well, folks, suppose Joanie had seen a Crisis Line flyer and called in."

"I'll role play Joanie, if that helps," Leanne offers, and begins. "Umm…I saw this number on a counselor's bulletin board at school. I hope it's okay to call. I'm thirteen years…My dad does nasty things to me…I tried to tell my mom. She doesn't believe me." She blows her nose.

"It's okay to cry," Jonathon intervenes. "Just take your time."

"She slapped me across the face, sent me to my room. Said I shouldn't spread such dirty, filthy tales about a man who is so good to us…"

"It must have hurt that she didn't believe you," Jonathon interjects.

"It did. I wanted to run away, but I can't. He'll just do the same thing to my little sister. She's nine. That's about the age I was…when he started."

"Could you handle that call?" Jonathon challenges the group.

Silence. Finally one weak voice volunteers, "No way."

"Then I guess we have a bit of work to do this afternoon," he says. "You'll need to know how the legal system handles these kinds of cases. And how you might support a victim locked in a terrible family situation."

As Carole processes Mary's story and the simulated call, she begins to understand how denial comes in many shapes and forms. Weren't her therapists locked into denial when they didn't want to know about a fellow therapist who was sexually active with his patients? Their unspoken message: *Don't talk about it. We don't care to air the family's dirty laundry. You're the crazy one. Let's talk about that.*

She raises her hand and asks, "Isn't it like incest when other caregivers abuse the people they are supposed to help? Like doctors, teachers, coaches, prison guards, uh, uh, therapists. Do sexual abuse laws cover them?"

Jonathan and Leanne exchange a sad look and a mutual sigh. "For minors, maybe," Leanne says. "For adults, not so much. We've been working on getting the laws changed. It's going to take a lot of consciousness-raising. I hear cases all the time. It's the hardest part of my job to tell victims we can't do anything but listen."

"We need the right case to grab public attention. Maybe one will come along some day," Jonathon suggests.

That evening Carole craves a razor blade to release the psychological pain that's been building up all afternoon. She chooses instead to journal.

*Would anyone understand that having sex with Jansen was one of the scariest things I've ever done. I remember being numb, so numb I wondered on the way home why I hadn't felt a thing. I just let him do what he said would cure me. Now I wonder if that couldn't be called the rape of my psyche. It damaged my soul more than my body.*

*Carpe diem. I will seize the day. I won't just walk away anymore. I'll recruit these two good people for my team. I will do the consciousness-raising Jonathon says is so badly needed. I will make it the focus of my master's program.*

She finally puts her journal aside, and sleeps more soundly than she has in years.

# 20

Helium balloons escape to high ceilings in the turn-of-the century Victorian home. Crepe paper streamers drape across the dining room, crown molding to crown molding. A sheet cake with thirteen candles adorns the dining room table. Lucy Jansen sits in her wheel chair, all smiles, a princess on her throne welcoming her many guests.

The smell of pizza in the making permeates the air when Harry Jansen arrives. He bends over to plant a kiss on his daughter's cheek. "You're beautiful, Sunshine, so grown up."

"Hi, Dad. I *am* grown up. I'm a teen now."

"You certainly are, honey." Harry turns away to hide the tears in his eyes. "Gotta go help your mom in the kitchen."

Giggles and laughter fill the room as the teens share whispered secrets they don't want him to hear.

In the kitchen, he finds Janine licking the spoon she just used to dish out the ice cream. Streaks of chocolate fudge swirl drip down her arm; she wipes them away on an old towel, before acknowledging her estranged husband's entrance.

"Hello, Harry." She glances at her watch. "Glad you could pull yourself away from work long enough to join us before the party's over."

"Look. I had an appointment. Besides, you know how I hate seeing Lucy's friends. She'll never have a normal life like theirs."

A look of annoyance spreads unchecked across Janine's face, but she chooses to ignore his provocative comment. "No fights," she says dismissively. "Not today."

Harry reaches for the whiskey flask in his pocket and places it on the kitchen counter.

"No, Harry," Janine says as she takes the flask and drains its content down the kitchen sink. "You are not going to drink in front of Lucy's friends."

"You just ignore what's happening to her," Harry complains. "I can't do that."

"All you ever see is the negative. Sure she's limited. She'll never walk. But she's bright and pretty and a lovely person to be around. Look at all the wonderful friends who came to her party. Can't you just focus on the blessings she brings into our lives. Always— always—it's the negative with you. I'm tired of it. Maybe *you* should see a psychiatrist." She spins around so as not to look at him before adding a final jab, "I won't let you spoil her day."

The front door bell interrupts the budding fight that never ends well. "I think that might be Ben," Maxine says. "You said he was coming. I'll get that."

"After all, he's Lucy's godfather," Janine explains. "I thought he might like to celebrate with us. Harry, you go entertain him. He's your best friend. He's got his own houseful of teens, so I'm sure he'd appreciate a little adult conversation."

Harry goes to the foyer, where he finds Ben carrying a bouquet of flowers for the hostess and a present for Lucy.

"Hey, Ben," Harry says. "We'd better stay out of the kitchen or they'll put us to work. Let's go out in the yard."

Ben hands the bouquet to Maxine to deliver to Janine as he responds. "First I want to see the birthday girl. I brought her a present."

"Uncle Ben," Lucy cries. "I'm so happy you came." She hugs her godfather as he leans down to plant a kiss on her cheek. "Now my day's complete."

"You look lovely. I brought you something." Ben offers her a small, rectangular package.

"That's got to be a book."

"How'd you guess? Am I that predictable?"

"You are, Uncle Ben. You always find me the best books to read. What's this one about?"

"You'll have to open it to find out, won't you?" Ben teases. "I can keep *some* secrets, you know."

"We've about demolished the pizzas. You'd better get some before it's all gone. Uh-oh, it's too late: here comes the dessert."

Ben smiles at Janine, who comes from the kitchen carrying a tray of ice cream sundaes. "Oh, I'll have one of those instead," he says reaching for a turtle sundae. "Let me take one to Harry. He's in the back yard."

"Thanks, Ben." Jannine's eyes sparkle with gratitude. She places the tray on the table and gives him a quick hug. "Go. He needs you. I can't be around him, not today."

# *21*

Carole shifts from being a quiet withdrawn patient to being a woman on a mission. The staff at County often find her working on class assignments in her free time.

She explains her assignment to an aide who stops by. "Our professor requires three papers of us about our dreams and visions that have matured over time. I guess it's her way of getting to know us better so she can provide us with appropriate guidance and support. She's kind of cool."

She holds up a draft of her first paper. "This is about an event that took place long ago."

*Thirteen cement steps lead up a grassy hill to the classic Victorian house I call home. On this warm autumn day, my brother and I sit on the steps of its wooden porch, awaiting the Halloween bewitching hour.*

*Our 75-year-old house would be a good setting for a Frankenstein movie, minus a Boris Karloff. Trap doors in the back yard lead into a dark, damp basement with a dusty coal bin, a dimly-lit cellar, and a large work room behind the coal furnace. The house also has a winding staircase that leads to an attic filled with all sorts of weird antiques. I have a wild imagination, so I mostly avoid both of those spaces unless I'm with someone else.*

*We neighborhood kids call the cream brick house at the end of the block 'the witches' house'. We always set up a lookout when we peer between the iron bars of the black grill fence at the three elderly women and their midnight-black cat. They're Frankenstein-eerie. We never go near them at Halloween. There's no point in taking such a frightening risk just for a candy bar!*

*My brother Paul and I talk while we wait for Trick or Treat time to arrive. Paul likes the tricking part; I like the treats. Mom says that's why he's always in trouble and I'm a bit chubby.*

*World War II ended not too long ago, so people are talking a lot about war heroes and superheroes.*

"Paul, do I look like Wonder Woman?" I ask my older brother. "Do you like my t'ara?"

"It's a tiara, stupid. Not a t'ara. Hmm...kind of, but you sure don't have her boobs."

I slump over to hide what's happening to me. I don't like that he knows my tiny breasts are starting to pop out. I hate the word 'boobs.' I think Paul learned that from the older boys he plays with. I hate the way my big sisters stare at me in the pool locker room and show me off to their friends. I feel like a freak. I can't help it if I'm growing hair down there. Why does he have to bring that up anyway?

"I love your Superman costume," I say, hoping to change the conversation.

"I look pretty good, don't I?" Paul stands up arrow-straight in his sky-blue long johns and red t-shirt. He extends his arms upwards as if to take off for the sky. The wind whips his yellow cape around. I can imagine him soaring far above the trees, and even beyond—to Krypton. He is Kal-El, the Man of Steel. I hope Mom won't be mad about him borrowing her curtain.

"Wouldn't it be grand if we were superheroes?" I ask. "Like the ones in your comic books. Mom says we can't have comics, but we all know they're hidden in your closet and under the bed." I giggle at our secret.

"Don't talk so loud, brat," Paul warns. "I don't want her to hear. You wanna start trouble?"

"You're naughty, Paul. Mom and Dad fight about you all the time. I think you like that. It makes you feel sooo important."

"I am," he grins. " I'm the only boy. And the best boy in the family." He likes to say that. It makes him sooo special. Three girls—only one boy! Big deal!

"It scares me when Mom and Dad fight all the time," I say. "I wish they were happy." I adjust the ill-fitting crown that's slipping off my head. "Wonder Woman's t'ara has magic powers. Maybe if I had a real one, I could fix things. Make them happy."

He says, "Doesn't bother me none."

I go on. "Those news reels...all that fighting! The guns! The tanks! The *bombings! People from concentration camps . . ." I shiver even though the October sun is warm. "I wish they wouldn't show us all that stuff. I wish you'd stop playing 'Bombs Over Tokyo' all the time. I wish people could just be happy."*

*"The word is 'tiara', stupid. Got it?"*

*I don't.*

*Then he says his piece. "That's a girl for you. Wimpy, wimpy, wimpy." Paul looks at me, scorn written all over his freckled face. "Hmmph. Wanna know how I'd take care of the bad guys? I'd send them flying out in space with one jab of my fist." Paul demonstrates his manly power with a punch to my upper am, one of his favorite targets. "That'd teach them."*

*"Mom says you're not supposed to hit me," I pout. Then I speak* my *piece. "Girls can be strong. And brave."*

*"Oh, sure," Paul sneers.*

*"If I were Wonder Woman," I insist, "I would be strong. I would have a magic bracelet and a golden lasso."*

*"Pfft. She's not as strong as* Superman.*"*

*I warn him to back off. "Someday I'm gonna find some Kryptonite. Then you won't hit me."*

*"Silly, there's no such thing!" Paul reaches out and snaps his finger sharply on the tip of my nose.*

*"Ouch, that hurt," I protest. "I like Wonder Woman. We're kind of like twins, both born the same year. She protects people from the bad guys. Some-day I want to do that, too."*

*I really believe that can happen. In* The Wizard of Oz, *I hear Dorothy sing about a place somewhere over the rainbow where dreams really do come true. Someday I'm going to find that place. Until then, I can help Mom with the dishes and sweep the floor and hang the wash to dry so she doesn't cry so much when Grandma starts a fight.*

*I straighten my plastic t'ara (way too big for my tiny head), adjust my stars and stripes, and swing my lasso. Today I am an Amazon!*

*My lasso plops on the ground with a thud. Guess I still have some grow-ing up to do.*

# 22

Finding Attorney Jonathon Prospect's building is easy; navigating traffic not so much, when thousands of people swarm downtown like worker bees vacating the hive. Carole finally spots the high rise.

She glances at the card Jonathon gave her. It says his law office is on the 8th floor. Carole feels conspicuous in an elevator occupied by professionals in chic business attire. Her fears are unfounded; no one even gives her a passing glance. By the time she reaches the 8th floor, everyone else has disembarked and gone their way. She steps into a legal office that occupies the entire top floor.

Everything has its proper place here, she notes: furniture aesthetically arranged, artwork color-coordinated, plants carefully cultivated, carpeting deeply-piled. A well-groomed receptionist looks up from her IBM Selectric typewriter, smiles, and directs her full attention to Carole.

"Can I help you?" she asks.

"Umm . . . Carole Thornton. I have an appointment to see Jonathon Prospect. Guess I'm a few minutes early."

"Ah, yes, I see you're next on his schedule. He's with another client but he'll be done shortly. Would you like to have a seat?" She gestures to the waiting area across from her desk. "How about something to drink while you are waiting? Coffee, tea, soda?"

Any liquid will help; Carole's mouth is bone dry. "Coffee, black; thank you."

Carole takes a seat in the waiting area and sips at the brew. Panic competes for her attention as minutes that seem like hours drag on. She should leave! She can make up some family emergency. What was she thinking? She'll never be able to tell her story to a man she barely knows.

She reaches for her purse, and rises to leave. Just then Jonathon strolls down the hallway toward her. Misgivings melt away as he smiles, extends a friendly handshake, and escorts Carole back to his office. When she glances out his window, people look like ants on the street below.

Jonathon takes a seat in a high-back black leather chair behind a finely-polished oak desk. It fits him well. Carole finds the client's chair unfamiliar and far less comfortable. After a bit of small talk, a prolonged silence ensues.

Jonathon loosens his tie, reaches for a mint, offers one to Carole. Then he opens the discussion. "Hey, relax, Carole. You're safe here. Whatever you tell me is confidential, you know. Attorney-client privilege."

"Yeah. I know. It's not that. I just don't know where to begin."

"As I recall, you wanted to explore legal options a person can pursue if he or she has been sexually exploited by a mental health professional."

"Exactly. But I can't pay." She hesitates to reveal her current status. "I'm a patient at the County Mental Health Center on leave from my job."

"Not a problem. I never charge for an initial consultation—office policy. Besides we don't even know if you have a case."

"True. I did something already though. I filed a complaint with the County Medical Society."

"The Medical Society can't do much, Carole. It's just an old boys' club. A physician doesn't have to belong to the Medical Society to practice medicine. Even if they expel him, it might sting his ego a bit, but who knows if they'd even do this much . . ." Jonathon demonstrates with a sharp slap on his wrist.

"So this was a mistake?"

"Not at all. But if I take your case, I'd expect you to consult with me about what you do. It works better that way for both of us."

"I thought it was a good place to start." Carole mumbles apologetically.

"No problem. I'll be interested to see how the Medical Society responds. But if you're looking for real professional oversight, the state department that regulates medical licensing has a lot more authority. Unfortunately, to date, they don't have a very good track record in this area."

"I sent them a letter, too," Carole mumbles.

"Good. How about you tell me a little more about your case, so I can decide if there's anything else you can do?" the attorney suggests.

She wishes she had a stick of gum. Her mouth is sooo dry. "This happened when I was in my early 20's."

Jonathan's legal brain immediately registers *statute of limitations.*

"I entered the convent at age 13," she begins. "At age 23 I left. Had a hard time adjusting." *Will he get what that was like for me,* she wonders.

"I'll bet. Catch-up time in so many ways. So how'd you connect with a therapist?"

"I first went to Sister Amelia, my college instructor in Developmental Psych, the only psychologist I had ever met, while I was in the convent. When I left the convent, we continued therapy for a while."

"Go on."

"I was finishing my bachelor's degree at the time. I shared an apartment with another patient of hers who had also left the convent. One day I came home from the university to find my roommate unconscious in bed. Someone had called the police. They banged on the door, questioned me, not too friendly. I knew nothing. Eventually they took her away in an ambulance. I learned it was a suicide attempt. Turns out she was pregnant, alone, and scared. Her mother had just died a few months before."

"And?"

"Sister Amelia was afraid I might be suicidal . . . a copycat thing, you know. I wasn't. She referred me to a psychiatrist who could prescribe medication. I didn't want to switch therapists but she insisted."

"Did she know the psychiatrist?"

"Guess so. She said she met him at a conference they both attended."

What Carole didn't know was that conference focused on the treatment of phobias. Sister Amelia attended the workshop on sex phobias. A fellow attendee—a Doctor Jansen—suggested, in spite of a universal reprimand from other professionals in the room, that therapy might provide a safe place for phobic patients to experience sex for the first time. Sister Amelia didn't rule out the psychiatrist's suggestion. In fact she kept his card for future reference.

"Sister Amelia recommended Dr. Jansen because he was a Catholic . . . said he would understand my convent background . . . said I needed a male therapist. Never said why."

Carole notes Jonathon is scribbling notes on a yellow legal tablet. She wonders if he thinks she is a real nut case. That's the way she feels.

"So when did the sexual activity begin?" Jonathon probes.

"About nine months into therapy. I was doing better socially so I began to trust Dr. Jansen. One day he asked me to talk about my first period. That unlocked a Pandora's box of pent-up emotions and unhappy memories. I'd never talked about that nightmare before . . . ever—and to a man?"

Tears well up in Carole's eyes. She's momentarily deluged in a tsunami of ancient origin—waves of fear, confusion, shame and embarrassment threaten to suck her under.

Gradually the flashback recedes.

"You don't have to go into the details about it now, Carole. It's obviously a painful topic for you. So you told him about it?"

"All the details. It was so humiliating. I thought he'd be disgusted . . . but when I looked up he was smiling at me. I just wanted a hug from him. I wanted someone to tell me I was okay."

She hesitates to go on, but she must.

"He took me on his lap. Like a father, I thought. Then he fondled my breasts. Called them wing buds. That was all that happened that day."

Jonathon grimaces, snaps his pencil so sharply it breaks. He reaches for another. "Carole, that was abuse even if he did nothing more. What happened after that?"

"During the next visit, he undressed me. This is so hard to talk about." Her voice falters. "We had sex for the first time. I don't remember everything. I do recall being naked on his avocado carpet.

That's about all. On my way home I wondered why I had been so afraid; I hadn't felt anything at all...That I do remember. I must have spaced out or something."

"Was that the only time you had sex?"

"In the following months he...we...engaged in sexual intercourse in every session except one." Carole rubs her hands across her eyes and forehead as if to wipe away the scarlet letter forever engraved there.

Jonathan keeps his tone as objective as possible, as an attorney should. "Did the sex ever take place outside of his office?"

"Never. I thought of it as *exposure therapy*. I'd heard about that. I really never knew what sex therapists did exactly." She blushes at her youthful ignorance.

She needs her attorney to understand, not judge. He's doing just that with his calm, factual approach. She pauses in her telling, then comments, "So that's what happened in a nutshell."

Jonathon sighs, appears to be lost in thought. Finally he breaks his silence. "There ought to be a criminal law to cover this. There isn't yet, but we're working on it. Sooo...my suggestion: file a civil malpractice suit."

That was something that had never occurred to Carole, and it didn't have any immediate appeal to her. This wasn't about money; it was about stopping further abuse. Her facial expression tells Jonathon he's going to have a bit of work to do to convince her.

"To stop this kind of abuse, we need to hit those who are getting away with it in the pocketbook where it really hurts. Ruin their reputation! That'll make them pay attention." He pauses. "Are you strong enough to handle a law suit?" he challenges.

Carole fingers her Wonder Woman pendant. There's no magic to this. She's got some work ahead of her. She'll take on the challenge not only for herself but for other victims out there.

"My life won't mean much if I remain stuck a victim forever, will it? My new therapist says I have to do something about what happened, if I want to get better."

"I'd like to talk to your therapist at County. I need to ask her if she feels you can handle a lawsuit. I think you have a viable case."

The attorney walks to the window, looks out at the tiny people rushing to and fro on the street below. After consulting his legal brain, he turns to face his client. "Our first hurdle will be the statute of limitations."

"So he might actually get away with this?" Carole asks.

"A strong possibility. I'll have to research legal precedents. Someone may have challenged that statute in a medical setting and won. That might take me a few days."

"So what can I do to help?" Carole inquires.

"Oh, there'll be plenty for you to do. Only you and Dr. Jansen know what happened in that therapy room. This will boil down to your word against his. You'll be the prime witness, though your current therapist will also be a key witness."

"Sounds like I'll be on trial as much as he is."

"You got it. I'm ready to take him on if you are," Jonathon offers, extending his strong hand to bond in a new partnership.

"I can't really back out, can I?" Carole concludes. "Not if I ever want to face myself in the mirror again."

# 23

There's no gentle way to purge Carole of the guilt that contributes to her ongoing depression, Dr. Schubachs concludes. So for today's session, the therapist plans a surgical approach; she will hurt in order to heal, like the physician who lances a boil to exhume the pus trapped inside.

Once her patient settles in, the therapist adopts a sharp accusatory tone. "My goodness, Carole, I'd think your religious background would have kept you from having sex with a married man."

Carole winces, glances first at the black and white floor tiles, then at the gray institutional door. "I wrestled with that ... prayed to the Holy Spirit for guidance ... went to Mass and Communion every day after work. Having sex was one of the scariest choices of my young life."

"It baffles me that you, a former nun, would do something like that."

Carole shifts uncomfortably as she defends herself. "What I learned about sex from the Church didn't make sense anymore. I needed help in sorting out my spiritual values. Instead of helping me do that, Dr. Jansen made fun of my beliefs. That made me feel foolish so I stopped bringing them up."

"Why didn't you turn to someone in the Church for help?"

"Are you kidding? My ten years in the Sister formation process were like a prolonged Marine boot camp. I'd had enough."

"What do you mean?"

"I needed to recover from a gross overdose of indoctrination. Guess that would be hard for you to understand...unless you'd spent your whole adolescence and early adulthood in a convent...The Doctor said sex would cure my depression. I believed him."

"Then why not talk to a girlfriend or your sisters?"

"The convent insisted we not discuss personal problems with our peers. I learned to keep my private life secret."

The clock ticks away precious therapy minutes. The 50-minute session is coming to a close. Schubachs decides it's time to abandon her accusatory tone, and to find out what became the tipping point in Carole's relationship with Jansen.

Carole's demeanor shifts as well. Guilt morphs into anger, like it did that day fifteen years ago. "He discounted me as a patient. When I asked him to hospitalizes me for my suicidal depression, he laughed, poured a drink and turned on soft music. That's when I wondered if I had just become a good lay for him? Had I become a whore, paying for my therapy with my body?"

"Quite a revelation, I'd say. That must have hurt."

"I was more angry than hurt...I'd grown so emotionally dependent on him...if anything that dependency was my bigger sin. I couldn't cut the bonds overnight."

"Your emotional dependence fueled his ego. He chose you because you lacked close friends and were pretty much alienated from your family. Do you get it?"

Carole straightens up, fingers her Wonder Woman pendant, announces in a strident voice, "I'm not powerless anymore."

The therapist glances at the clock. This hour has been well spent. At the sound of a door opening and shutting, she prepares herself for another patient with another problem. Schubachs wheels her chair over to a file drawer where she withdraws the lengthy bibliography on sexual abuse by therapists that Carole developed from her library research.

"I looked this over. Great articles. You were going to look for articles about how people recover. Did you find any?"

"No." Carole's shoulders droop at first, but then she straightens tall. "I think people recover when they stop being a victim," she concludes.

Carole spends long hours working on the assignment for her Leadership for Change class the following week. She realizes that her class project might actually become a blueprint for what she plans to do to fight sexual abuse by therapists. She identifies change agents who might help her achieve that goal, and suggests strategies to engage their interest. When she turns her paper in, the professor writes in the margin "A+ I hope you follow through and make this happen."

Her healing journey begins to take shape.

# 24

Dr. Harry Jansen is on his fifth drink by the time his friend arrives at the pub. He straightens up from his sprawling position when he spots the attorney in the doorway, and knocks over an empty glass in the process. "Over here, Ben" he calls out.

"Sorry I'm late," Ben apologizes while loosening his tie. "Got tied up with a court case. Divorce can be so messy."

"Tell me. Been there, done that."

While Ben heads to the bar for a Coke, Harry counts his blessing. Nothing like having a lawyer buddy to fall back on in a pinch.

"DUI or speeding?" Ben asks when he returns.

"Worse. I got *this* in the mail." Harry fumbles for the letter in his coat pocket. "Need your advice."

In shadows cast by a flickering candle, Ben makes out the official letterhead of the Medical Society. He scans the content not once but twice. Impossibly stupid. Even for Harry. "What? You had sex with a patient? During therapy? That's really low."

"Lower your voice," Harry cautions. "You want the whole world to hear? Did it for her own good, man. A convent dropout. No sex experience at all! She needed some education."

"An ex-nun yet?" Ben grabs a napkin to wipe up Harry's mess. "Aw shit, Harry. You lost a wife, the loveliest woman a man could ever wish for. You've got a daughter who adores you. Why'd you go and do this? Sex with a patient? Shit! I'm tired of cleaning up your messes. Don't know if I can rescue you this time. This . . . this could cost you your career."

Jansen stares at a mesmerizing neon sign. On, off. On, off. On, off. On . . . off.

"Happened a long time ago, Ben." Jansen responds, as if that is some kind of excuse. "Then out of the blue, THIS!" His liquored breath causes Ben to draw back in disgust.

"Sober up, damn it. How do you expect me to advise you until I know the facts."

"Don't be so God-almighty sanctimonious. Got your own secrets, mister."

"You got me through finals back in the day, when I was hung up on LSD," Ben replies. "I've more than paid you back. We're not college mates anymore."

"It was sex education. Why if I hadn't intervened, she'd probably be some dowdy old maid or even a homo by now. She ought to be thanking me. I'm good with women. You know that, Ben," he grins.

"Still the high school jock? Your charm is long gone, lover boy," Ben counters.

"I'm the psychiatrist, not you, you prick! She needed hands-on experience, not just empty talk."

"So, you gonna tell *that* to the Medical Society? I hope you have solid research to back up your treatment plan..." Ben counters in a voice thick with sarcasm.

"Assholes...they'd never buy it."

"Course not! Doctors don't have sex with their patients. Ever hear of the Hippocratic Oath? We may have been college mates but I'm not sure I wanna defend you this time. If it weren't for Lucy..."

Now the neon light catches Ben's attention. On, off. On, off. On...What a regrettable choice that was, letting Jansen take his finals years ago. How much longer until that debt gets paid off?

Jansen modulates his tone. "Come on, Ben, you old fart." Jansen grabs his friend's wrist. Ben pulls away.

"Enough. I need to use the men's room."

"And I need a drink."

Ben barks over a departing shoulder, "Coffee—black. Get your head together so we can carry on a rational conversation!"

"A cup of black coffee at that table," Ben tells the barkeeper, handing him a generous tip. "Make it strong, *very* strong."

Ben stalls in the restroom corridor, allowing time for his client to sober up while he cools down. He catches up on a few business calls, then telephones his wife to excuse his delay.

Hoping the java has worked its magic, he approaches Harry armed with his best legal advice. "Resign from the Medical Society. It's just a professional organization. No one has to belong. That should halt their investigation."

"Hey, that makes sense," Harry says. "I knew you'd have an answer, buddy."

"Let's hope that ends it. But if her complaint reaches the licensing folks..." Ben pauses to let that worst case scenario cogitate in his client's mind. "Think she—what's her name? Carole Thornton— would go that far?"

"Not the Carole Thornton I knew. The kid I knew wouldn't have complained to anyone. Too naive and way too scared."

"Well, Harry, people change. She's complaining now."

Jansen trades bravado for looming defeat. "No proof. It'll be my word against crazy Carole. Eventually she'll cave in. You'll see."

It's not a hangover that ruins the rest of Dr. Jansen's day. It's a disturbing message on his answering machine.

"Call me, Jim Anderson, lead investigator with the State Licensing and Regulatory Department. I'd like to meet with you to discuss a letter we received from a Carole Thornton in your office sometime next week. My number is..."

"Bitch!" Jansen collapses in his recliner, then frantically dials Ben's number.

The answering machine drones, "Please leave your name, number and a short message..."

"Ben. Damn it. Pick up the phone. Come on, come on. Pick up!"

Ben breaks in, "What's the freakin' crisis?"

"The bitch complained to the State!"

"Shit!"

"Some investigator, a Jim Anderson, wants to meet next week!"

"I've got to get to court now. Don't do anything 'til we talk. I should be in your neighborhood this afternoon. Four o'clock ok?"

"Fine."

Jansen hangs up. Out of habit he reaches for a whiskey bottle hidden in the lamp stand, and downs a few slurps.

He adjusts the recliner to an upright position, stares across the room at a phantom Carole, a figment of his intoxicated imagination. "Why the hell didn't you just come to me? We could've settled this between us. Money... How much you want?"

Nothing.

"Revenge?" he yells. "That what you want? Want me publicly flogged? How about a pound of my hide?"

"I want to get better," she responds. "That's all I ever wanted." She slips away.

Jansen retreats into his own dark soul where memories of the past still haunt him.

*"Your mother can't go to Communion like the other parents,"* Sister Angelina *announced in front of the whole class. "She's divorced and remarried."*

*Mom cried when I told her — the only time I ever saw her cry.*

*Didn't much care about my First Communion after that. When Aunt Susan gave me a Rosary, I threw it in the creek. The damn thing got entangled in some rocks. Neither time nor raging flood waters ever worked it loose. I'll bet it's still caught there.*

"Fuck you, Carole. You're just another Sister Angelina—come to do me in!"

Suddenly the phantom patient returns…glares at him.

"You should be thanking me. Purged you of all that Catholic crap…at least I tried," he shouts.

Silence.

"Why are you so pissed? You needed a letter when you wanted to marry 'cause the priest wondered if you were mentally fit. I laughed right out loud at that arrogance on his part! Who put them in charge of people's lives? I told you…find a justice of the peace! When you insisted, I sent your damned letter. Had to have the blessing of the Church…after all the things they did to you? Pathetic!!"

Angry eyes glare back at him.

"So the damned Church still has its hold?"

He shrugs and processes that thought. "Now I get it! You're on some kind of mission. Still out to right the world's wrongs, are you? Thought I fucked that out of you."

The phantom smiles, fades away.

"Bitch!"

A distant church bell chimes the four o'clock hour. Ben composes himself on the couch in Harry's office while his client paces erratically around the room…to the windows overlooking a central courtyard, to the bookcases that line the opposite walls, past the waiting room door, back to the windows...

"Probably the best legal strategy, just admit what you did." Ben suggests.

Jansen spins around outraged. "You crazy?"

"Surrender your license for a year or two. If you lie, and they prove you're lying, they'll throw the book at you," Ben warns. "They'll make an example of you."

"Stop that. You're my lawyer. It's your job to get me out of this."

Ben rolls his shoulders back as he physically and psychologically rejects the weight Harry just dumped on him. "I'm not a defense attorney. I may not be the best one to advise you. This isn't just a complaint to the Medical Society anymore."

"I saved your ass!" Jansen shouts. "Your time to save mine."

Ben mumbles. "Never let me forget, do you?"

"Not gonna admit *anything*. Got it, Ben?"

"This could potentially become a civil malpractice suit," the lawyer speculates. "If I were her attorney, that's where I'd be heading with it. That's totally not my area of expertise. Then, like it or not, you'll have to call in the big guns."

The sullen look on Jansen's face suggests he expects a different answer.

Ben proposes a compromise. "How about I do the grunt work? At least let me consult with a malpractice attorney."

"Can't afford them. Besides, you owe me. I want you representing me!"

"Okay, okay." Ben sighs. "I have to know where we stand though. Are there others out there? I probably don't want to know."

"What?" Jansen's head jerks back. He glances around the sound-proof office to assure himself no one can hear what he has to say. "Confidentially, right? Lawyer-client privilege?

Ben nods.

Jansen admits, "Could be."

Ben groans. "So others could come forward?"

"They won't want the publicity. Believe me."

"I have to be prepared."

"Look, Ben, I figured out Carole's motive. She's on a mission to save the world."

"Hmm…ex-nun—makes sense. Your worst nightmare: a Wonder Woman on a mission!"

"Betcha someone out there's pushing the agenda. She'd never do this on her own. Pretty sure I can make her cave in."

"How?"

"I'll come up with a way."

"Get back to me when you've figured out how. Meanwhile set up that appointment with the investigator. See what they have on you. The burden of proof still rests with the State."

"Carole's plain crazy. That's my defense."

# 25

Betty Schubachs is first to arrive at the Twilight Café. Its well-worn wooden tables and rickety floors are familiar and forever trendy. She orders a strong cup of fresh roasted coffee, then maneuvers to a booth where she can keep an eye out for Dr. Peale. Voices echo loudly in the hollow spaces of the old room. A lively ethics debate in the back corner of the popular student hangout takes her back to an earlier time.

*School days, school days/ Dear old Golden Rule days.* The world was black and white back then. Debating ethical issues was fun, energizing. Today, there's no more black and white. Just shades of gray, and her choices impact people's lives, not her grades.

The sight of a familiar black Cadillac pulling onto the parking lot interrupts Betty's musings. As Dr. Jerry Peale enters, she waves to draw his attention. He approaches, tosses a mound of papers on an extra seat, then sits down across from his colleague.

"Thanks for coming, Jerry. Not the fanciest spot but there's a bit of privacy. Plus I love the energy here."

"My kind of place, too: busy, noisy, clean. Best of all, the coffee's strong."

"Can I get you some?" she offers.

"No, thanks," he sighs. "Meetings stacked on meetings today. I've exhausted my caffeine quota for the day."

"I need to talk to you about Carole."

"What about her? She seems to be doing well enough in group."

"It's what's going on outside of group. You know she reported sexual contact with two previous therapists in her intake . . ." Betty sighs. "I'm not sure how to advise her."

"Something happen?"

"I pushed Carole to do something about what happened." Betty throws up her hands in consternation. "She's taken it on as her mission in life. I don't know where it's all going to end."

Dr. Peale backs away. "I don't like getting involved in a colleague's treatment." The desperation in Betty's eyes causes him to reconsider. "Like it or not, I guess I am involved. Seeing as Carole's in our group therapy . . ." He raises his eyebrows quizzically. "What did you expect her to do exactly?"

"Nothing in particular. Talk about it . . . think about it . . . whatever."

"Do something about it? That's a challenge, albeit a pretty vague one." Peale strokes his gray beard and asks, "So what's she done so far?"

"Filed two complaints—one with the Medical Society and one with the licensing folks."

"Whoa," he blusters. "Where'd she get that idea? Not from you, I hope."

Betty is not prepared for Peale's knee-jerk, highly-animated response. She withers before his apparent disapproval. "Not exactly my idea. She's got connections at the university. And she can find her way around the library. I guess she did a bit of research."

Their conversation is interrupted by a loud crash coming from the kitchen. The shattering of the institutional crockery brings the cafe buzz to a halt. The manager is heard swearing at the culprit. Within seconds, the rather uncomfortable silence passes as a diligent waitress steps over the fallen debris and delivers food to pacify the hungry customers.

In the brief conversation that follows the crash, Schubachs learns a lot about her colleague. She discovers Peale will protect his profession first, his coworkers next, any patient—a distant third. He shares information about a public relations nightmare discussed at one of the meetings he just attended: the Mental Health Center is under scrutiny for a report of sexual improprieties.

"There'll be hell to pay when the licensing folks come snooping around," Peale cautions in a subdued tone. "Slim chance the complainant can prove her accusations. Others couldn't." He pulls back from the table, set on ending this discussion. "Careful you're not labeled whistleblower. Your involvement in this kind of case will play right into the hands of those men who covet your position."

"For heaven's sake, we can't keep pretending this isn't happening. It's the 1980's, Jerry. Don't you think it's time to do something about abusive therapists? They give us all a black eye. The best PR would be to demonstrate concern."

"You'd better do some real soul searching! I wouldn't sacrifice my career for *ANY* patient. Don't let this get out of hand, Betty."

Betty returns to her car a bit disillusioned. She mumbles, "Just keep quiet—but that approach just eats away at you. I know. I've tried it in my own life."

# 26

Carole was admitted to the Mental Health Center on a foggy February day. It's a sunny June day when she's released as part of an unexplained massive discharge on the unit. New artwork and freshly potted plants suddenly appear there even as the patients depart. Rumor spreads: the hospital accreditation team will be paying a visit.

Three omens of impending doom heighten the unit's anxiety. The Pope has just been shot by a political dissident. The unit is on alert due to a bomb threat. Speculation is that Manic Mike once again off his meds called in the threat. A howling siren warns of an approaching tornado. It's a mad, mad world—not safe inside or out.

Four-year-old Jack eases Carole's tension when he races toward her in the lobby with open arms. "Mommy, Mommy. Your doctor gave me a birthday present. She said you can come home."

Carole shifts into mommy gear, reaching down to scoop him up. "Happy Birthday! Let's have a picnic to celebrate. Potato salad, baked beans, and strawberry shortcake for my Strawberry Kid. Daddy can grill burgers and hot dogs."

Awakened by thunder late that night, little Jack calls out, "Drinko!" Carole brings him a glass of water and the assurance his Mom is still around. She tucks him in and plants a gentle kiss on his forehead. His older brothers, now also awake, call out for their drinks. She delivers water to each of them along with the confirmation that she is now home for good. The house quiets down. Her sleep is disturbed only by Arvid's snoring, a gentle assurance that tonight at least all is well.

# 27

Carole wakes up a bit later than the rest of the household. She grins at the warm sounds of home life: the bickering for dibs at a new Batman comic, the buzzing of an electric razor, and the chit-chat of the early morning news team. Home is a far better place to be. She promises herself there'll be no more hospitalizations.

Arvid leaves for summer school classes. The boys take off for games with the neighbor kids, for bikes, sandbox play, and a dip in the wading pool. She knows they'll check in for food and the periodic reconciliation of the predictable petty conflicts the day will bring.

She decides to spend her morning restoring order to the house in total disarray after her prolonged absence. "Where to start?" she murmurs out loud. "Maybe clear the front entry so people can actually get in?" Footsteps on the porch catch her attention. The mailman, of course.

In sorting through the mail, she notes incoming bills from the Mental Health Center. She sighs at the financial burden that will haunt them for months, probably years to come. When she spots the logo of the County Medical Society, she places the envelope against her heart and whispers a quick prayer before slitting it open. Stunned by its content, she dials her attorney. Jonathon picks up on the third ring.

"It's Carole," she mumbles.

"Morning, Carole. What's up?"

"A letter just came. Dr. Jansen resigned from the Medical Society. They claim they have no more jurisdiction over him."

"Hmm...smart move on his part," Jonathon responds. "I'd have advised him to do that."

"Their letter states, 'the State will follow through with an investigation of Dr. Jansen and he will not escape their jurisdiction as easily.'"

"Interesting comment."

"Isn't he kind of admitting he did something wrong? Why else would he resign? Doesn't it sound like they believe me?"

"Don't read too much into it, Carole. They're pissed that he ignored their process." Then he adds, a bit cynically, "They're probably relieved to turn jurisdiction over to some other entity anyway."

"Oh," she responds, disappointment in her voice.

"Look, Carole, the Medical Society's response is of far less consequence than what I have to tell you. Remember what I said about the statute of limitations? That we couldn't get anywhere unless the court chooses to view your case in an unconventional way?"

"You mean if I would file a civil case? Money's not what I want out of this."

"I get that. You want to be taken seriously. I do, too. But be practical, Carole. Money talks. Civil law suits draw public attention to unprofessional behavior. Isn't that what you want?"

"Yes. Of course I do. But going for his license—that's another way to stop him."

"Not to disillusion you, but the licensing folks in this state have yet to rein in one single abusive therapist. Even if Jansen were to lose his license, he could just move to another state and practice there."

Carole taps her fingers on the kitchen table in tempo with the wall clock. Tick, tock, tick, tock, tick, tock. Time is passing; maybe it's already too late.

"At least listen to what I have to say," Jonathon says. "Then decide."

"I'm listening."

"The statute of limitations is a legal strategy to force people to act in a timely manner. Fifteen years have passed since this happened. Legally you should have filed a civil law suit long ago."

"My bad, I guess. I was duped. I didn't know it was malpractice."

"Exactly. That's what I've been mulling around in my head."

The attorney clears his throat, as men do as their way of announcing they have something important to say. "I searched for a precedent—some case where the court interpreted the statute more broadly."

She stops breathing, gulps in air, and whispers, "Did you find one?"

"I did."

Jonathon outlines the case. A patient complained of severe abdominal pain many years after surgery. Follow-up treatment discovered a surgeon left something behind in his stomach cavity. The judge ruled the countdown for the statute of limitation kicked in when the source of the pain was discovered, not when the original malpractice occurred.

Her mind races ahead. "I get it. You'd argue I couldn't come forward until I discovered psychiatric malpractice, which happened when I did my library research at the university. That's when I found what Jansen left behind—so to speak."

"Exactly. Dr. Schubachs can testify to that."

"Whether or not you can pursue the case depends on the judge we get," Jonathon cautions. "A liberal one, I hope." He pauses as he weighs the likelihood of ever getting a day in court. Then he adds, "But if we win, your case could set a precedent for other victims of abuse. They're out there, believe me."

Carole hears whispering on the other end of the line.

"Sorry. I have to take an important call. I need to put you on hold. Meanwhile think about what I said. It's a long shot but I'm willing to take the risk if you are."

As the minutes pass, Carole's attention is drawn to a bumble bee pollinating a rose bush just outside her kitchen window. She'd hate a world without roses. Maybe she could become a pollinator, like the bee. Funny, though, how beautiful roses always come with thorns.

When Jonathan returns, Carole reports her reasoning. "If someone doesn't confront this abuse, it'll just go on and on, won't it?"

"Do I hear a yes?" Jonathon asks. "We can go ahead then?"

"I was naive, very dependent. I've grown beyond that. I want other victims to know they can move on, too." She pauses, then adds, "We can become survivors, instead of victims," speaking in a confident voice that belies the uncertainty she feels.

Jonathon explains that he will file a $4 million dollar civil malpractice suit, which he hopes will garner media attention. Carole gulps at a sum she cannot even imagine. Money enough to buy the kids better clothes, to put savings away for their college, to pay off medical expenses—intriguing, but such daydreams are quickly crushed by the voice of reason that cautions, *That's just La La Land.* The chance of ever telling her story in civil court is marginal. But even a remote chance is better than none.

"I'll sign the forms," she says. "What else do you need from me?"

"When you're assigned an attorney by the State, I'd like a waiver that allows us to share information."

"I'd like that, too."

# 28

Carole agrees to meet Jonathon at the County Court House for the initial hearing. Arriving well in advance of schedule, she studies the antiquated room. Along with a handful of observers, she sits on well-worn wooden benches behind a barrier that separates the crowd from the main players on the stage. The judge is elevated above all others. A court reporter sits to his right, positioned to hear and record all exchanges between the judge and the opposing attorneys. *Just like in the movies*, she thinks.

Ignoring the case currently in play, she notes a gigantic mural on the wall: the blindfolded Roman goddess Justice holds a balanced scale in her hand.

It reminds her of the cultural images of justice portrayed across the ages. Justice never had a blindfold until the Age of Reason displaced emotion as a judicial consideration. Themis, her Greek predecessor, favored restorative justice. The Hebrew God promised Solomon, an icon of scriptural fame, "I will give you a heart so wise and understanding that there has never been anyone like you up to now."

She wonders if her judge will be Justice, cold and legalistic? Themis, compassionate and reconciling? Or Solomon, wise and understanding?

When Jonathon brings her case to the bench, the process lasts but a few brief minutes. She sees each lawyer submit a brief. The judge glances in her direction once, but his conversation with the attorneys is out of hearing range.

Afterwards Jonathon fills her in on what happened in the short exchange. Jansen's attorney, Ben Tisch, filed a $6 million dollar libel suit against them, claiming Carole's lawsuit to be frivolous.

Carole blanches. A tsunami of emotions momentarily engulfs her. Lost in its deluge, she eventually selects laughter for a lifeline. "You can't get water from a stone, as they say. Where would I get six million dollars? We can hardly meet our $550 monthly mortgage."

Anger surges in her belly at Tisch's suggestion that the case is frivolous. There is nothing frivolous about this; she is dead serious.

Her attorney explains it is legal terminology that refers to a case that is a waste of the court's valuable time since it can't possibly go forward. Jonathon and his law firm could be penalized if the judge were to rule the case frivolous. There are penalties for filing frivolous cases. He doesn't appear too shaken, though. He calls their motions "saber rattling."

While waiting in line at the grocery store a week later, Carole spots a glaring headline on the front page of a tabloid newspaper: "Ex-nun Sues Psychiatrist for Sexual Abuse". The story inside is merely a couple of inches long and never mentions her name. Nevertheless, it makes her feel naked, exposed. The public scrutiny of her private life has just begun.

She purchases a copy of the paper, tucks it deep in one of the paper grocery bags, and slinks her way to the car. Once home, she slips it into her dresser so Arvid and the children will never see it. Will she be able to deal with what is about to happen? How will it affect her family?

# 29

Weeks of stewing end when Jonathon invites Carole to his office to share the court's decision. His body language tells her the news is not all positive.

"In a nutshell, you will not have your day in civil court. The judge applied a conservative interpretation of the statute of limitations. Sorry, Carole."

She accepts with grace, but inquires about the ruling on whether or not the case is frivolous.

"Well, the judge labels Jansen's behavior 'heinous.' It's a ruling based solely on the statute of limitations. He did not consider the case frivolous."

Carole is relieved that her attorney and his firm will not be punished for taking her case. She asks about her own financial liability.

"Nothing to worry about on that score. I told you it was just saber rattling. Once off the hook, Jansen dropped the $6 million libel suit."

She shrugs. "Money to pay for my hospital bills and future therapy would have been nice, but what I really want is for him to take personal responsibility for what he did. I want him to tell the truth, man up, maybe show some remorse? He sure didn't."

"Don't expect that," Jonathon cautions. "You'll be badly disappointed if you do."

"At least now I know what I'm up against. I see more clearly just what kind of man he is. I can cast aside any loyalty to him that still lingers," Carole shares. "Maybe that's a part of the healing process..."

Jonathon sees a look of sadness on his client's face. He doesn't know what to say as he watches her face head-on the betrayal of the trust she once placed in her therapist.

Not wanting to take up anymore of Jonathon's time, Carole gets up to leave.

"Thanks for taking my case. I saw substance in your argument, even if the judge didn't. I guess this means you're not my lawyer anymore, huh?"

"If you'll have me, I'd like to continue to provide any legal help I can, maybe consult with the state attorney assigned your case."

"But I don't have money to pay you..."

"I'll gladly do this pro bono. I want to stay involved. We've waited so long for a case like yours to come up."

"Thank you," she says with tears in her eyes.

"You can count on Leanne's support, too." Jonathon assures her. "We're both part of your team. We're in for the long haul."

In parting, he quotes Charles de Gaulle: "France has lost the battle; she has not lost the war."

# *30*

Life goes on; Carole's getting used to picking up the pieces. The very next day, she meets with her university advisor to discuss her next plans.

Portraits of Gloria Steinem, Susan B. Anthony, and Betty Friedan decorate the walls in Dawn's office. The pleasant aroma of lavender-scented candles and a blooming African violet modify the institutional setting, creating a warm woman's space. Dawn welcomes Carole with a cheerful hello.

"Come. Sit. I just read the paper you wrote for the Leadership for Change class. I'm impressed with the action plan you developed. It's excellent."

"Thanks. I hope someday my plans will materialize."

"I'd put my money on it, Carole."

Carole glances at the smiley face in the margin. So much has happened since she wrote that paper. She has to think twice about what those strategies are. She vaguely recalls a long laundry list of things she plans to do.

Dawn offers her support. "I can help you. You've already met dedicated feminists at the Crisis Line. I have another important contact for you: Catherine McGilligan, a real ball of fire. Besides her work with NOW, she served on President Carter's Advisory Committee on Women. She's an influential voice in the Statewide Women's Network, too. If she takes you under her wing, she can connect you with other pioneer women."

Carole takes the business card Dawn hands her, then shares a project already in the works. "A social worker from a woman's health collective wants to do a story on sexual abuse by therapists for their newsletter. She promises to protect my identity."

"Great way to start. You'll get help from women in the Network, too. These 1980's feminists are less inclined to burn their bras. They're better engaged in crafting legislation that affects women's lives. The Network has a direct line to the Governor's ear through a woman he appointed as his advisor on women's issues. She can help, too. You need to get her attention."

What began as a fluke of an idea grows in intensity. Carole volunteers for the curriculum planning committee of the annual Woman to Woman conference that draws thousands of women from around the state. With Gloria Steinem as Sunday's keynote speaker, this year's conference is sure to attract media attention. Another plus. In her volunteer role, Carole approves a workshop on sexual abuse in therapy to help her reach activists who will support her efforts.

Her plan works. Women who attend the workshop agree to meet after the conference to strategize for further action. Members of the group—including two women psychiatrists, a representative from the Mental Health Association, and other survivors—identify an immediate goal to establish a support group for survivors who might come forward as the topic receives public attention. They exchange contact information and plan to keep in touch.

On a Sunday morning two weeks later, Carole opens the local newspaper, pleasantly surprised to see a prominent female journalist has written a one-page feature story on therapist sexual abuse.

"There's someone else out there!" she exclaims as she holds up the paper for Arvid to see.

Looking up from the sports page, he asks, "Where? In the yard?"

"No. No. Silly. Look. A full page article about therapist abuse . . . with artwork and everything."

"Anything new?" he asks.

"The woman they interviewed wants to remain anonymous. But she's talking, and people are listening. Her representative just proposed a change to the state sexual assault laws that would make sexual contact between a therapist and a patient a felony."

She saves the paper, excited that change is on the horizon. Monday morning she calls Leanne to share her enthusiasm. The social worker invites Carole to testify about her experience at a public hearing scheduled before the legislative committee in the state capitol later in the week. She agrees to do so.

While Carole's public persona appears strong and confident, stress takes its toll on her. The day before the public hearing, in the secrecy of her own bathroom, she slashes her abdomen with a razor blade multiple times, releasing the psychic pain fermenting inside. She knows better than to let anyone else see it. They'd never understand. She washes away the blood with a cotton ball, then walks into the living room where Arvid is watching a baseball game.

"Shall we take the kids to the park?" Carole suggests.

Leanne is first to testify at the hearing. She expresses the frustration members of the District Attorney's office experience when complaints come in, but nothing can be done under the existing sexual assault laws unless the complainant was psychotic at the time of the abuse. She suggests that the proposed bill would give them the tool they need to investigate and prosecute offenders. Carole follows, offering a victim's perspective.

She learns firsthand how laws get passed and how they get stalled. While she expects opposition to the bill from mental health professional organizations, she is surprised when a lobbyist for the Catholic Church opposes the bill. Why in heaven's name would the Church oppose it?

# 31

Upon her arrival at the student union a week later, Carole finds the usual beehive of activity, with students swarming around as they eat, study, visit or network. It's as good a place as any to kill time before her scheduled meeting with Investigator Jim Anderson from the State Licensing Department. She spots someone from her evening class, and wanders over to her table.

"Is that you, Henrietta?" Carole whispers in her classmate's ear. "You look so studious."

"You here, too? This hour of the day? Sit. Could sure use a break about now." She extends a half-empty bag in Carole's direction. "Have some chips?"

"Thanks, too nervous to eat anything."

"Hey. My turn to be nervous. My presentation's tonight. You finished yours already."

"You'll do fine, Henrietta. I'm nervous for another reason. I'm about to meet the investigator assigned to my case." Carole shivers though the room is not cold.

"Oh my, I'd be nervous, too. You must really believe in what you're doing to take on something like that." She places her dark-skinned hand on Carole's arm. "You're brave, Carole. I'm with you all the way. We women, we stick together."

"Why thank you, Henrietta."

"I'm curious, Carole. Do you have any plans for what you'll do after you get your degree?"

"Don't know yet. Maybe work in an organization that empowers women."

"Sounds like a perfect fit to me."

"How about you, Henrietta? How do you plan to use your degree?"

"In community health. We surely need better baby care in my community. Our little ones got to get a better start in life."

"I know you'll be good at it." Carole glances at her watch. There's just enough time left to find the meeting room. "See you tonight." She rises to leave. "I'll let you know how this goes," she promises in parting.

Henrietta raises both thumbs up as Carole leaves. She returns the salute.

As Carole turns down the hall leading to the meeting room, she spots a tall, handsome stranger in his mid to late thirties carrying a leather briefcase. It has to be the man she is supposed to meet.

When she approaches, he introduces himself, presenting an ID to verify his status with the State Licensing Agency. Why he's the very image of Sergeant Joe Friday, she says to herself. Jim Anderson is here to get the facts—just the facts, ma'am.

He opens the door, steps aside to let her enter first. "Did you have any trouble finding the place?" he asks Carole.

"Not at all. I attend class here."

Carole sees a long conference table in the windowless room illuminated by bright florescent lights. So like an interrogation room on TV.

"Sit wherever you'd like. Make yourself comfortable."

She suggest her Joe Friday take the head of the table while she sits along the side. When both are settled in place, the investigator opens his brief case and withdraws a manila folder.

"We've read your complaint about Dr. Harry Jansen. My job is to piece together what actually happened for Attorney Abe Friedman, who's been assigned to handle this. Finding evidence is a bit challenging in cases this old, but I'll do my best."

The specter of the statute of limitation looms again in Carole's mind. "Not impossible, I hope."

"First, it would help if you have receipts to verify that you and Dr. Jansen had a professional relationship," Jim begins. "We need to establish that right up front."

"Hmm…my parents paid the bills. They might have the cancelled checks." Carole knows her father is a bit of a hoarder, so there's a chance he might still have them. She cringes as she realizes she's going to have to tell her parents what happened back then. No parent could be happy to hear their money was spent on medical malpractice.

He makes note of her comment, then moves on. "You mentioned that Dr. Jansen gave you gifts. Do you still have them?"

"I have the electric shaver he bought…an amulet of Estée Lauder perfume…a book entitled *David and Lisa*." She hesitates, embarrassed to bring up more personal items. "I'm afraid I threw away the lingerie. It's not the kind I prefer." Carole blushes. She relates how Jansen had tossed the box it came in across the room for her to catch. When she opened it, she thought the scanty pink and orange paisley lingerie was a gift for his little girl. No, he wanted her to wear it. She felt squeamish when he eyed her in bikini panties, a far cry from her convent undergarments.

Jim clears his throat, embarrassed at her embarrassment. "Sorry, I have to ask you these questions."

"I get that."

"Did you meet Dr. Jansen anywhere other than in his office? At a hotel ? At your house? At a bar or a restaurant?"

"Only once. I had a car accident. Someone sideswiped me on a side street after dark. My black Falcon was pushed into a building, completely demolished. The police took me to a hospital as a precaution. I was released, but I had no transportation home. This was my first accident, so I was pretty shook up. I called Dr. Jansen. He picked me up at the hospital, gave me medicine to calm me down, then dropped me off at my aunt's house. He never came in."

"Was there any other time you were with him outside the office?"

"Just once. I came for my regular therapy session. He told me he just bought a red Firebird convertible. He wanted me to ride with him to the lakefront and back. I did what he asked. We were gone ten minutes at the most. We came right back to the office for my regular therapy session afterwards."

Jim continues to scribble notes. "You mentioned he gave you alcohol during the sessions. Can you tell me about that?"

She explained how Jansen always had a bottle of Jack Daniels stashed in the lamp stand next to his recliner. Though he'd encouraged her to take some, she declined, never having developed a taste for liquor. So he brought Champale for her instead, which he cooled over the air conditioner blower. She'd drink a little of that.

"We visited Jansen at his office," Jim says. "We have reason to believe he's an alcoholic. He seemed intoxicated, and possibly hooked on some kind of drug."

Carole is pleased to hear they have visited Jansen. They are taking her complaint seriously.

"Do you remember your diagnosis?" Jim asks.

"I do," Carole says. "*Adjustment reaction with depression.* Labels just stick in your head. I hate them. They box people in. I'm not some label. I'm me."

"Good memory. That's in his records. He can't argue you were psychotic, that's for sure. We know he prescribed Elavil for depression and Valium for anxiety. Any medications besides that?"

"Hmm . . . yeah, birth control pills. At the time, only married women could get the pill, so he'd prescribed them for his wife, go the pharmacy, and then he'd give them to me instead."

"Now that's not in the records."

"I wasn't having sex at the time. He gave them to me to reduce acne on my back. I was young and struggled with that like most young adults."

Jim looks over his glasses, taken aback at Carole's naivety. "Maybe that's what he told you. I'm sure he had something else in mind. You're fortunate he did that. Pregnancy would really have complicated your life and his."

After an uneasy pause, she confesses with chagrin, "I was really stupid, wasn't I?"

"Desperate, naive, not necessarily stupid. When we're young we often do dumb things we regret later in life."

That small touch of humanity makes it possible for Carole to continue, even though the room is beginning to spin and the fluorescent lights are glowing brighter and brighter. In the windowless room, moving air is at a premium.

"Did you ever tell anyone?" Jim continues. "A sister? A friend? Anyone?"

Carole squirms. "Mind if we take a break? I need water and some fresh air."

"Okay. Meet you back here in a half hour."

Air, water, and Henrietta's friendly face, that's what she needs. She gets all three in a brief sojourn at the student union. When she returns, she plumbs her memory for an answer to Jim's parting question and she finds something. She dated a guy back then. She told him she was seeing a psychiatrist and having sex with him. It was a cry for help that fell on deaf ears.

Jim looks up. He's paying attention now. "Name? Address?"

"Not sure. Fifteen years is a long time ago. All I remember is he was a teacher in the suburbs who lived with his mother on Catalina Boulevard."

Jim wrote down the information. "If I can find him, he could be our corroborating witness. Think hard, Carole. Did *anyone* else know about this?"

Carole scrunches her forehead as she revisits the late 1960's. "Hmm . . . let me think. Nobody. Nope."

Suddenly she perks up. "Wait. I told a priest I was seeing a psychiatrist. I confessed to having sex with a married man but I never mentioned the married man was my psychiatrist."

"Wish you had," Jim sighs.

"He required a letter from my psychiatrist to certify I was fit to marry in my current mental state before he would officiate at my wedding."

"Not a typical requirement." Jim shakes his head in befuddlement as he considers the irony of the whole situation. "So what'd you do?"

Carole explains she got Dr. Jansen to write the letter under protest. Perhaps it is still in the church records. Jim suggests it might be hard to retrieve if it does still exist, since clergy guard church records as carefully as they do the seal of confession.

She shakes her head sadly when Jim suggests maybe she talked to a girlfriend or a family member. He speculates Jansen might have picked her just because she was so isolated and easy to manipulate. That will make his job even harder.

"I just remembered someone else." Carole recalls in an excited tone. "I told my family doctor."

She then describes how it came up during her first pelvic exam.

She reported having had sex with her therapist. Her GP's response was puzzling at the time. He said that man did her a grave disservice.

When she returned years later after losing seventy pounds for no reason, he told her she was being totally consumed with anger, which made no sense at all, since she felt depressed and anxious, not angry.

"I'll need that family doctor's name and address," Jim responds.

"Unfortunately he passed away recently," she says. "I'll get the address of the clinic where he practiced. He might have put something in his medical records."

"I'm also going to need the names and addresses of all the therapists you've seen over the years and a signed release of information form that give me permission to speak to each of them. About how many would that be?"

"Boy..." She starts to count their names on her fingers. When she runs out of fingers, she replies, "Must have been at least twelve or thirteen."

"And no one suggested what Jansen did was wrong? Wow."

Jim sits back, balancing his chair at a precarious angle. Something is gnawing at him. Finally he blurts it out. "Why'd you go along with Dr. Jansen anyway?"

"I'd heard about *exposure therapy* in my psych class. Therapists sometimes expose people to things they fear like riding elevators or flying in planes. I thought if I was exposed to sex, I wouldn't be so afraid of it. I was young and stupid, I guess."

Jim assures her she was conned by an expert. Then confides his own feelings. "My little sister is seeing a therapist. If he ever took advantage of her in the vulnerable state she's in...why, I'd want to kill the guy." He shudders at the very thought of such a dastardly deed.

That personal reaction triggers something in the investigator's head. "Maybe I should question Jansen's ex-wife. Wonder what she could tell me about her husband's brand of therapy?"

Jim looks at the forlorn figure across the table, and sighs. "Don't you give up. I'm good at what I do and I've just begun!"

He then gathers up his papers, a signal that the interrogation is now over. "Enough for now, Carole. Abe or I will get back to you soon."

As he exits the room, he reminds her not to forget to send the therapists' names and signed release of information forms.

Henrietta is pacing nervously when Carole arrives for their evening class. She pauses to hug her classmate, then insists on a report. "Well, tell me how it went. Good, bad?"

"The investigator believes me. That's good." She smiles half-heartedly, then her expression shifts. "He told me the doctor denies ever having sex with me. That's bad."

"Of course he denied it," Henrietta says, pulling back. Having grown up in the inner city, she has well-honed street smarts, something Carole sorely lacks. "You're gonna have to toughen up, Carole. The world is full of people like him," she adds.

"But the world is also full of people who are kind and good and generous. Like you, Henrietta," Carole whispers, with tears in her eyes.

Henrietta hugs Carole a second time. "I don't always succeed, girl, but I surely do try. Makes me angry and sad…all this bad stuff happening to you."

The room is beginning to fill. Carole takes a front seat eager to offer Henrietta moral support as her friend gives the evening presentation. It's the least she can do.

# 32

That night, not wanting to disturb Arvid's sleep, Carole lays as quiet as her restless mind permits, but after hours of insomnia, she finally tosses her covers aside and tiptoes to the kitchen where she fumbles in her briefcase for her journal. Just like an investigator, her psyche is engaged in trying to piece together what happened back then. She captures her state back then in a poem:

Doors
lead out
lead in
standing on the threshold
jammed with doubt
visions
memories collide
in an emotional bout
what is this exit
entrance all about?

Dr. Schubachs is also finding it difficult to sleep these days. So much so that she feels the need for a professional consultation. She chooses to meet with a prominent female psychiatrist at a cafe far from the hospital. Before the two sit down, she orders a cup of java from the man behind the counter.

"I'll take the same," Dr. Bemmer says, "and one of those," she adds, pointing to a blueberry muffin in the display case. "For here."

Space is plentiful mid-afternoon, and they select a booth in the back that offers the privacy they seek.

Schubachs much admires Dr. Marjorie Bemmer, a feminist icon in the psychiatric community. At times, she dreams that someday she will secure a partnership in Bemmer's clinic. For now, she wants her as an ally.

Tossing small talk aside, she quickly cuts to the chase. "I suppose you're wondering why I asked to meet you." Her voice cracks. She clears her throat and steadies her resolve.

"Please, call me Marjorie," the older woman suggests, lending a less formal tone to their meeting.

"Of course. I'm Betty."

"I have to admit, I am a bit curious," Bemmer says. "We don't know each other very well, but I know you have a teaching position at the Medical College. Does this meeting have something to do with that?"

"What we have in common is . . . umm, we're two professional women trying to make it in a man's world," Betty begins. She's rehearsed her speech many times, but somehow it sounds stilted when she says the words out loud.

Marjorie chuckles. "I think I'm way beyond that, Betty. I've been doctoring for decades, before you ever dreamed of going to medical school. I've my very own clinic. The world belongs to those who seize it. That's my philosophy, and it's paid off."

In the face of Betty's apparent discomfort, Marjorie softens her tone and reaches out to touch her hand. Betty pulls back.

"That doesn't mean I've forgotten what it was like to be the only female psychiatrist in the old boys club," Marjorie says. "My gender was constricting. Probably still is; though in my own private practice, I can be whatever person I want to be."

Betty sighs. "I'd love to have your . . . freedom. I don't."

"What's up?"

"I'm in a bit of a bind. A patient told me two previous therapists engaged in sexual behavior with her during treatment. I think she needs to deal with that abuse if she ever hopes to lead a normal life. Otherwise, she could be headed for a lifetime of institutionalization or worse. This is her third hospitalization in two years."

Marjorie tells Betty she knows the person in question, having met her at the recent Woman to Woman Conference. She approves of Carole's approach to addressing the problem.

"I like what Carole's trying to do," Bemmer says. "She's into research, planning and then action. That's what it takes, and in that order."

"She's taking off like a rocket, well fueled by a pent-up rage. You probably read about her lawsuit. It made the papers recently."

Marjorie nods, "I did."

"She's become a spitfire I can't contain?" Betty complains.

"Why would you want to quell such enthusiasm, Betty? Her case might actually move the issue of sexual abuse by therapists to the forefront. It needs to be taken seriously. In the good old boys' network, it's just a joke."

"But, but...she filed a complaint with the State Licensing Board." Betty begins twisting her napkin. Visions of them snooping around have haunted her ever since her conversation with Dr. Peale.

"Kudos," Marjorie responds. "A woman of action. I'm behind her on that."

Betty stutters, "But you're not—you're not her therapist. I am." She gasps for air before raising her concerns. "Don't you get it? *My* career is at risk. So is my marriage."

"I'm listening."

"If word gets around that I put her up to this, I won't be very popular with my male colleagues." she says, wiping her clammy hands on her skirt.

Betty's not about to tell Marjorie of the nondisclosure agreement she made with the college when she was bartering for her current position. She sold a part of her soul that day. She's not proud of what she did; she plans to take *that* secret to the grave.

"Marjorie, the last thing I need is to be seen as a radical feminist, or even worse, a *whistleblower*. I don't have tenure. I can't afford to lose my teaching position. My husband is unemployed right now. We need the income."

Betty searches Marjorie's dark eyes for some small sign of compassion. There's none in her steel gaze.

"We women have to take unpopular stands if we ever hope to change society," Marjorie says. "You can't advise your patient to do something and then remain aloof and uninvolved. You're gonna be drawn into this, Betty. You up to that or not?"

"People respect you, even though you're viewed as a feminist, Marjorie. What's your secret? I'd really like to know."

"Well, first, you need to know what you're talking about. That's where research comes in. When you achieve clarity, you need courage to follow your convictions. Then you find people of a like mind to support you. And by the way, I'm willing to support you—and Carole—in any way I can."

"But, but...she's not ready to deal with what lies ahead any more than I am! She's going to be on trial more than he is."

"Glad you understand that, Betty. That's exactly why many victims don't report sexual abuse. But your job is to support Carole. That's the commitment you made when you accepted a patient with that background."

She hesitates to scare Betty but feels the younger woman needs to understand what lies ahead for her as a key witness. "Be prepared to have your life scrutinized, too. They'll try to discredit you, too, you know."

Ignoring the anxiety that sweeps over Betty's face, Marjorie encourages her to be more proactive. "Move to the forefront on this," she suggests. "Aren't you in charge of the quarterly lecture series? Make sexual abuse by therapists the topic of one in-service."

"Hmm...I hadn't thought of that."

"We've been hiding this dirty, dark secret too long," Bemmer says. "It's time to expose it. The mental health community is going to be more attentive now. A bill has been proposed that will make sexual misconduct by a therapist or counselor a felony in this state. Believe me, they'll be listening."

Betty Schubachs wrestles with her options. Could she lose her job if she does as Marjorie suggest? She's sacrificed everything to get where she is. Every morning she wakes up thrilled to be making it in a man's world. She needs the money to support her family and pay off student loans. Jake's meager UC check isn't cutting it.

"It's ground-breaking work we're doing, Betty." Marjorie says. "You up for it?" she challenges her a second time.

Betty is caught up in indecision. Life on the fence has always been so debilitating and of late it's become a habit she can't seem to shake. She knows she's definitely not the Wonder Woman Carole aspires to be.

# *33*

Across town, Attorney Ben Tisch parks his Cadillac in the downtown parking structure and takes the elevator to the eighth floor. He has a message to deliver his client, one he knows will not be well-received. His stomach grows increasingly more queasy when he enters Jansen's office and finds him pacing. That's never a good sign; neither is the smell of liquor on his client's breath.

"Shit," Jansen tosses aside the paperwork Tisch proffers him. "Don't hand me this legal mumble jumble. Just tell me. How we doing?" He pours himself a shot of Scotch, offers one to his attorney.

"Sober up, Daniel. When liquor talks, no one really listens."

"What's up?" Jansen asks, as he gulps the whiskey down "Where do we stand?"

"I'm afraid you're gonna need the big guns after all. It'll cost, but losing your license will cost you a whole lot more."

"Can't afford them," Jansen puts his arms around Tisch's shoulder. "Buddy to buddy, what would you suggest?"

Ben squirms away from the taller man to create a professional distance between them. "I'm no expert on this kind of thing, but in my opinion you'd come out ahead if you cooperate with the State. Work out some agreement—say, agree to an impaired physician stint."

A half-soused Jansen resorts to whining. "Those jerks with their hypocritical oath. Probably fucking their patients, too. But *they're* gonna discipline *me*. Make *me* the fall guy?" He reaches for the whiskey bottle.

Frustrated by Jansen's cavalier attitude towards very serious charges, Tisch heads to the door.

"Whoa! Come on back here, Buddy." Jansen puts the bottle away. "So, all right, tell me. How do I *cooperate* without admitting I did it?"

"To begin with, turn over her records..." his attorney suggests.

"Did that. What else?"

"Then...admit to what you did," Tisch finishes.

"Shit! No way! That's a dead end."

"If you contest it, you better find yourself a good character witness. You'll need it."

"Not to worry. I got lots of friends. I know their secrets, like I know yours." He winks at his attorney. "Someone will testify. I guarantee."

Ben shoulders droop. How he'd love to walk out of this disempowering relationship! But the only way out is to finish the case and quit. One last favor should even things out between them.

"If you still insist I represent you, at least let me consult with a malpractice expert," he mutters.

"Damn it, go ahead, but don't agree to anything until we talk."

# 34

D r. Schubachs scarcely notices the bright blue cloudless sky as she parks her car at the Mental Health Center. She's suffering from battle fatigue after the fight with Jake last night, so she reaches for more caffeine to fuel her for the long, boring day ahead.

Jake crossed a line when he demanded not only a divorce but child support and custody of the kids to boot. How dare he accuse her of being an unfit mother so wrapped up in her career that she has no time for them. Why, he doesn't even have a job! Not too responsible there.

Then to claim the *crazies* she works with pose a danger to the family? Her crazies pose no more of a threat than angry people he laid off before the company moved south. She remembers the anonymous phone calls in the dead of night. That was no picnic in the park.

This is turning into such a dirty divorce. How's she supposed to focus on her patients when she can't even get a good night's sleep?

Schubachs groans as she checks the day's calendar. Carole, first on the day's docket, will be there bright and early, she surmises. She steps out of the car, straightens her skirt, and glances at her well-manicured nails as she checks the time on her Lady Rolex, before picking up her pace. She's a bit late.

"Morning, Carole," she says, passing an anxious, obviously distraught patient pacing in the hall. "I'm running a bit late. Give me a few minutes?"

"Sure, Dr. Schubachs," Carole responds, relieved that her therapist has arrived. "Take your time. I'm not going anywhere."

The therapy session begins with Carole's legal update. She shares her disappointment at the judge's ruling on the civil suit. Blah, blah, blah. She whines about the $6 million dollar libel suit, goes on and on about her recent interview with the state investigator, blah, blah, blah. It's getting hard for Dr. Schubachs to keep from dozing off . . .

When the patient mentions *Lovesick*, a movie that has just been released, her therapist tunes out. She has no time to keep up with the latest movies and has no idea what it's about.

Carole explains it's about a therapist who falls in love with his client. She shuts her eyes, her shoulders droop. "How can they make a comedy out of that?"

She waits for her therapist to say something. Nothing is forthcoming. No word of compassion or understanding or at least some acknowledgement that Carole might find the subject of the comedy offensive. Nothing.

Carole wipes aside tears, opens her eyes to glance at her therapist only to discover Dr. Schubachs is sound asleep! She reaches for her purse and her sudden movement awakens the therapist.

An embarrassed psychiatrist lashes out at her patient. "If you had something important to say, Carole, I might find it easier to stay awake."

Carole stands up, pulls out the razor blade she always carries in her purse. The flow of blood will make the pain more visceral, *real* in a world that chooses to ignore its existence.

"Wake up. See. My pain. It's real. It hurts," she screams as she slashes her arm. The cut scarcely breaks the surface, but it's deep enough to cause blood to flow. She streaks out of the room, races down the hall, and heads for the parking lot.

The scarcely alert psychiatrist pushes the panic button, then gets up to pursue her patient.

By that time Carole is already out the door. She fumbles with her car keys, drops them on the pavement, picks them up, then fumbles again. Finally she manages to open the car door. As she places the bloody razor blade on the dashboard and prepares to drive off, she spots a county sheriff in her rear view mirror and Dr. Schubachs exiting the building.

The motor of her ancient Comet doesn't turn over fast enough, so she abandons the vehicle to seek an alternative escape route. She weaves her way on foot across a four-lane road jammed with workaday traffic. Carole mounts a grassy knoll, seeking sanctuary in one of the abandoned buildings at the top.

The county sheriff, much faster and much younger and far more athletic is in pursuit, never taking his well-trained eyes off his target. He grabs Carole just as she's about to lose herself in the institutional maze.

He throws her face down to the ground, handcuffs her arms behind her back, and sits on her awaiting further orders. He laughs at her resistance and pulls hard on the handcuffs, drawing more blood from her open wound. "Bitch!" He mutters in her ear. Carole feels a hardening in his crotch.

In high heels, Dr. Schubachs is at a great disadvantage in the chase. When she finally catches up, she orders the sheriff to take Carole to the emergency room. "Get her wounds treated. Then put her on a locked unit. I'll take it from there."

Then she turns and stomps away. "Damn you, Carole Thornton, you make me look like a fool in front of my colleagues," she mutters as she treks back to the Mental Health Center. "How will I ever explain this?"

Once Carole's superficial wounds are treated in the emergency room, the sheriff escorts her to the Mental Health Center. "Want my advice?" he leers, rolling his dark eyes. When Carole fails to respond, he offers it anyway. "There's nothing wrong with you that a good fuck wouldn't cure."

Carole bites down on her lip until it begins to bleed. He just confirmed what she suspected. It was an erection poking at her back when he mounted her. And now he just uttered the very words Jansen used when she begged to be hospitalized for her deepening depression.

Back on the unit, she breathes a sigh of relief; she is safe. The sheriff relates his version of the morning events to the staff in the nursing station. In another part of the building, Dr. Schubachs tells her story, never mentioning how she'd fallen asleep during Carole's therapy session.

No one hears Carole's version. Could anyone really understand what it feels like to have the world laugh at a lovesick therapist? Or how it feels to be treated as a sex object while handcuffed to an armed officer of the law?

She hears the sheriff whistle his way down the hall as the locked door swings shut behind him. Carole spends the night inside, for the first time confined to a mental ward against her will.

When Dr. Schubachs signs the order to release Carole the next morning, the psychiatrist scarcely looks at her. "We'll talk more about this at the next group meeting," she says. "I hope you got my message. I have the legal power to lock you up. Don't you ever forget that."

When Carole returns to her car, she sees her razor blade still sealed to the dashboard by her own blood, an ugly reminder that her rage can still geyser out of control. What triggers these meltdowns? What accounts for her disconnect from the human race? Why does she feel abandoned and adrift in a turbulent sea with no lifeboat to cling to? Will these volatile episodes never end?

# 35

Carole has an appointment at the Sensitive Crimes Unit that very day. She welcomes the distraction from the wrenching events of the past twenty-four hours. She breathes slowly and deeply, squelching her anxiety as best she can, then reaches for her Wonder Woman talisman. It takes a superhero to ward off supervillains. Sometimes those villains lurk right inside.

She rubs the pendant to summon forth her better self. Thinking it best to avoid future temptation, she wraps the bloody razor blade in layers of tissue and disposes of it in a trash can. She resolves to never carry one again.

Not wanting anyone to see evidence of her recent meltdown, Carole grabs a sweater from the back seat, puts it on to hide the fresh cut on her wrist. She then takes off for downtown.

Fifteen minutes later Carole enters the rather foreboding administrative building. She walks slowly past guards armed with revolvers and bully sticks. Once inside, she discovers a complex maze with ugly gray walls, ancient well-worn wooden benches, and very official names stenciled on opaque glass doors. Following posted directions, she finds the Sensitive Crimes Unit located within the wing that houses the D.A.'s office. The receptionist there is friendly, mid-thirties, attentive.

"I have an appointment to see Leanne Summers. My name is Carole Thornton."

"I'll let her know you're here. May be a few minutes though; she's in a meeting now. Would you like to take a seat over there?" she gestures. "Can I get you something to drink? Water, coffee, soda?"

"Thanks, I'm okay."

Carole people-watches while she waits. Lawyers coming from legal proceedings stop at the receptionist's desk to exchange high fives, or to swear at an unyielding judge. The receptionist celebrates or commiserates with them, as she handles incoming calls, and still receives visitors with grace.

A woman clothed in profound sadness shares the waiting area with Carole. Her toddler, dressed in clean clothes, her hair meticulously braided and locked in place with colorful ribbons, clings to her mother's knee for grounding. While the mother appears spaced out, the child is very much present to what is going on. Carole engages the little one in a game of peek-a-boo. Innocent giggles provide a much appreciated relief for both of them.

Eventually, Carole spots Leanne coming down the long hallway. A welcome sight. She waves goodbye to the little girl who smiles while burying her face in her mother's lap. She gets up to meet with the Director of the Sensitive Crimes Unit. Finally, an ally she can count on.

"It's good to see you again, Carole," Leanne says. "Let's go to my office," she suggests.

The office is rather frugal, as befits a governmental unit, but with personal touches that warm the dreary space.

She begins by acknowledging Carole's loss. Jonathon had told her the civil suit didn't go anywhere. "I'm so sorry about that. I know how much you wanted your day in court."

When Carole's face register regret, she adds, "Your case did serve a purpose though. It got the media's attention. Other victims might come forward. There are others out there, you know. By the way, how is your support group doing?"

Carole perks up. She's very proud of that group. "Great. We've given ourselves a name. There's only three of us so far, but we're making some noise."

"Two lawsuits made the paper recently. Are those women from your group?"

Carole's eyes sparkle. "Both are pursuing civil law suits. And their cases are moving forward." She raises her right arm in the victory punch of Rosie the Riveter. "They don't have to fight the statute of limitations like I do."

Carole elaborates. "One woman is very strong. She'll do fine. I'm more concerned about the other—she's married, very pregnant with her therapist's baby. At times she disassociates—finds herself in unfamiliar places, but can't remember how she got there. Her mental state is affecting her health, her marriage, her family, her job. I hope not the baby in her womb. The two of us support her as best we can. Luckily, her therapist is Dr. Bemmer."

"Woman-to-woman supporting each other, that's the way it's always been. You're opening doors for others. These are difficult cases, but I don't have to tell you that. You already know how draining they can be. Your time will come, too, Carole. Some day you'll be heard."

"FYI, five women have shown up here with complaints about abusive therapists. All we can do is listen, and that's just not enough." Leanne sighs. Her eyes tear up.

"Listening helps, believe me," Carole assures her. "I've spent decades just trying to get someone to listen." She then inquires about a newspaper report that the County Mental Health Center is currently under investigation for patient sexual abuse. She asks Leanne if she is involved in this case.

"Sorry, I can't discuss an ongoing investigation."

"Okay. Speaking of County, I learned through the patient grapevine that Manic Mike, someone I shared the unit with, who sang Irish shanties so loud we couldn't sleep, was abused by a priest as a young seminarian. After our mass discharge, he called in the fake bomb threat."

"Ouch." Leanne sighs. "It's hard for a man to admit being abused."

"It's even tougher when you're a mental patient in a county institution with a long DUI arrest record," Carole adds. "Plenty of fodder to discredit you there. Who wants their dirty laundry aired in public?"

The phone interrupts their conversation. Leanne is wanted elsewhere.

She glances at the clock. "I'm going to have to cut this short. I'm due in court soon." She stands up to leave. "I'll be there for you, Carole. I promise. Jonathon and I plan to come to your hearing. We know how hard it is to talk about such personal matters in a public arena."

While walking Carole down the hall, she apologizes. "I wish I could offer victim compensation to cover your therapy expenses, but since the existing criminal code doesn't cover that abuse, you don't qualify. One more reason to change the legal code."

"I never expected money, Leanne. You've been a big support in more important ways." Carole leaves the office three feet taller, now reenergized for the task that lies ahead.

# *36*

Carole takes a break from motherhood and the law suits to enjoy lunch with her grade school friends Darlene and Barbara. They know nothing about her hospitalizations or her lawsuit, and that's the way she plans to keep it. Some things one just doesn't share, even with the best of friends.

"Remember how we stood on the church corner talking for hours on end?" Darlene chuckles as they settle into a restaurant booth in their old neighborhood. "The Three Musketeers, that's what Father George used to call us."

"My Mom said we wore a groove in the cement walking each other home," Carole reminisces. "We sure did find lots to talk about. With party lines back then, there's no way we could tie up the telephone. Someone would get mad at us."

Darlene, in a stylish hat, still wears the prim and proper demeanor her petite Italian immigrant mamma instilled in her bambinos. Barbara was raised in a Scotch-Irish family. With her bright red hair, pretty clothes, and outgoing personality, she was the most popular girl in class. It helped that her father owned a downtown restaurant and knew lots of important people, including the city's major league baseball team.

Carole once envied the breakfast of hot chocolate, hard-boiled eggs, and a meat sandwich Barbara's stay-at-home mom packed for her. She, on the other hand, had to pack her own peanut butter sandwich and throw a couple of Danish Delight cookies in a brown paper bag herself, since her nurse mom was off to work before she even got up.

The three had gone their separate ways after grade school, but on occasion they got together to remember old times and to share updates on where life was taking them now.

"Hey, Darlene, remember how we wanted to be like Sister Mary Clare? We were going to save the world. Both of us planned to enter the convent right after grade school. My parents were okay with me going. Your mom said no, not 'til after high school. Oh, the plans we made. Here we are—neither of us in the convent anymore. Guess we've found other ways to 'save the world.'"

"That's one thing we all got from the nuns," Barbara interjects. "A determination to make this a better world in our own way."

After an enjoyable visit, they hug and say good-bye, once more going their separate ways. By the time Carole arrives home, summer's late afternoon drizzle has morphed into a thunderstorm. The tat, tat, tat of golf-ball-sized hail on the windshield ends her childhood reverie. Could there be a tornado be in the offing? Emergency signals are not screaming out a warning, but still an alarm is going off in her head. She is seized by a premonition that something bad is about to happen.

First off, she checks her phone messages. Her mom delivers devastating and unexpected news in a calm nurse voice. "Dad's being admitted to the hospital. The pancreatic cancer has metastasized. It's in one of his lungs. He's going into surgery early tomorrow morning."

Five years have passed since Dad's cancer was first diagnosed. Carole's reaction to his illness lodges somewhere between irritation, empathy, and grief. He's just kept right on smoking in spite of the physician's warning. He has a reservoir of excuses, as most addicts do. "Rule out smoking," he insists. "My cancer is the result of being exposed to chlorine gas at work."

Chemist that he is, scientist he claims to be, still he ignores the lethal toxins he inhales each time he lights up. "Doctors who smoke choose Camels," the ads claims. So does he.

Carole's mom promises a call back when she has more information to share.

Next on the machine, a call-when-you-can message, followed by a phone number for the state's attorney, Abe Friedman. Carole dials the number. When Attorney Friedman answers, he suggests she hang up so he can call back at the state's expense, since she is now a state witness and taxpayers should foot the bill, not her.

After social pleasantries, Friedman gets to the point of his call. "I spoke with Jonathon. He told me about the judge's decision in the civil suit. Sorry to hear you'll not get your day in court. I'm certain you'll get a hearing with us, if that helps any."

"Thanks. Someone has to wake up the sleeping giant to what is going on."

"I guess you two did that all right. Multi-million-dollar lawsuits have a way of catching public attention."

Abe clears his throat. "Jonathon asked to consult on the case. I'm fine with that. He won't have any formal jurisdiction, this being a State matter now, but he can advise you along the way."

"Good."

"Here's the update on what's happening on our end. Jim found Damion, the teacher you dated back then. Damion remembers you but he doesn't remember any conversation about a psychiatrist. Either it never made an impression on him, he has a bad memory, or he just doesn't want to get involved. Jim isn't sure which it is, but suspects it might be the last."

Carole flashes back to the 1960's. Damion had an impact on her life; it's a bit disappointing to learn she had so little on his. Maybe he really didn't hear her. She tends to speak softly when she's scared. She probably slipped into her mousy voice that day.

In a kind of an in-your-face warning, she'd reported her conversation to Dr. Jansen. The psychiatrist laughed it off. His invincibility cut her back down to size. Feeling totally discounted by him and by Damion, she determined never to discuss the sexual activity with anyone again. So when she met Arvid a few months later, she never mentioned it. She wasn't going to take a chance on losing him, too.

Abe's voice brings Carole back to the present.

"As far as getting Church records, that's going to be a challenge. The priest who counseled you remembers you said something about an affair with a married man, but you didn't tell him the married man you had sex with was your psychiatrist. He had an uneasy feeling about your state of mind. Father, now an ex-priest by the way, wanted to make certain you were psychologically fit to marry. He does remember a letter from Dr. Jansen. He thinks it might be archived at the chancery, though he's not sure."

"As for the other priest, the one you talked to more recently, he's claiming the seal of the confessional. He refuses to even discuss your case with us."

"Really? We talked about it in his office, not in the confessional. Maybe if I ask, he might be willing to talk. If I had his number…"

"I'll have Jim send it to you."

Abe continues. "Jim and I are going to see the nun therapist who referred you to Dr. Jansen next. You said you returned to her with your concerns a few years later. She could be an important witness in our case."

How ironic that Sister Amelia, the nun psychologist who once meant the world to Carole, would be the one to actually hold Carole's future in her hands once again. It was Amelia who had advised her to leave the convent, who had been a mentor, a role model, and a support, even a mother figure to her.

But the nun had stepped over a professional boundary in her treatment, and the psychologist had to be stopped, too.

"The Psychology Board received your complaint about her," Abe continues. "They're a different entity; they'll follow through separately. I know you'll want to know what happens. I'll call you after our meeting. Hopefully the nun will tell the truth."

"Sister Amelia is at least twenty years older than I am, Abe. I'm not sure if that relationship was maternal or predatory, or possibly a mixture of both."

"I'll know more when I talk to her about what she did," Abe sighs. "Do you think she'll own up?"

"I have no idea." Carole's shoulders sag with dread and uncertainty. "She might. She's not like Dr. Jansen."

"Not to change the subject, but I read the interview you did with the reporter. He never mentioned your name, but I knew it was you. Good article."

"Thank God the paper's policy is to withhold the name of a sexual assault victim. I have to be careful. Arvid teaches in an ultraconservative suburb. If my name goes public when the case moves forward, we could have a problem."

"We could request a closed hearing to safeguard your privacy."

"Thanks, Abe. But I vacillate between the need for privacy and the public's need for transparency. We'll see."

Carole glances at the kitchen clock that's ticking away her Dad's limited hours on earth. "Guess I'd better get off the phone in case my mom's trying to call. My dad's set for surgery tomorrow."

"I hope things work out. Talk to you later."

Mom's call finally comes, but not until the next day. The news is not good. The surgeon had to do an emergency tracheotomy after the surgery.

"Can he have visitors, Mom?"

"A few at a time. He's sedated and can't talk, of course." Her voice breaks. The silence that follows says more than any words. Eventually she regains her mom-in-control voice. "I know you have to make arrangements for the kids. Just come when you can."

"Be there after supper."

Carole retreats to her bedroom for a short nap. She dreams of a gigantic snowball gaining momentum as it crashes down the mountainside, destroying everything in its path.

What does this foreshadow, she wonders upon awakening. She brushes aside the anxiety clinging to her subconscious to prepare supper for her husband and kids. As soon as Arvid gets home, she leaves for the hospital.

While driving across town, it crosses her mind that Arvid's been distant of late. Is he pulling away, or is she so wrapped up in her own problems that she cut off their communication? Perhaps tonight she better check in with him, after hospital hours and beyond the ears of inquisitive kids.

# 37

Abe and Jim head out the following morning to interview Sister Amelia, a key witness in the case. They cruise along the bucolic miles between the two cities at a comfortable pace and beat the lunch crowd to a roadside café, where they stop for a bite to eat. A few breakfast leftovers, mostly retired men, linger at the counter sharing local gossip, pontificating on political trends, and prognosticating about championship chances for their favorite teams.

"We'd better take a remote table where we can talk more freely," Abe suggests. "Loose lips sink ships, as they say."

Both men settle on the special of the day: chicken dumpling soup, a house burger, and a Pepsi beverage at a price well within the lunch allowance for state employees on the road. Once they place their orders, they address the business at hand.

"Eighteen therapists," Jim mentions as he tests the steaming bowl of soup that arrives shortly. "That's how many Carole's seen. You'd think someone would have reported something a lot sooner."

"Nobody could see that many," Abe replies. "Some *must* have been auxiliary personnel. I'd focus on her primary therapists."

"I've read through their files. She consistently reported a sexual relationship with a former therapist to Family Service, Catholic Social Services, West Haven Psych, St. Mary's, St. Anthony's . . . the litany goes on. Many recorded her claim, but they all treated it like a minor footnote. No one really delved into it. Not until Schubachs." Jim shakes his head in disbelief.

Abe, who tends to eat faster, pushes his soup bowl aside, commenting, "Classic denial. Who likes to point a finger at a colleague anyway?"

Jim coughs as cracker crumbs catch in his throat. When he recovers, he says, "What? . . . easier to bury your head in the sand and do nothing?"

About then the waitress shows up with the burgers. "It's our specialty, guaranteed to please." She waits for feedback. The first bite elicits Jim's grunt of approval.

"Told ya they'd be good," she smiles, then moves away.

"So what would you do if one of your coworkers was sexually involved with a client?" Jim asks when she's out of reach of his voice. "Think you'd report it?"

"Hmm . . ." Abe mulls over the question before he gives a definitive answer. "As professionals we deal with vulnerable people every day. We process lots of confidential information ... maybe ... knowledge is power, as they say ... haven't had to face that yet. Hard to say what I'd do. Guess I wouldn't be a happy camper if anyone ever put me in a position where I had to report him. Or her."

Jim tolerates Abe's non-answer. It's typical of his boss to weigh his answers to challenging questions very carefully. They finish eating in silence.

After finishing his burger, Jim pushes aside his plate and resurrects the conversation. "Sister Amelia is both a therapist and a religious figure. Carole had a double reason to trust her."

"And a double reason to feel betrayed," Abe adds.

The attorney glances at the clock. "Guess we'd better get on to the nunnery. To be honest, I'm not looking forward to this conversation with Sister Amelia, but we need to know how she will respond if she's to be our witness. I can't leave that to chance. If she admits to her own abuse, it would make our job a lot easier." He taps his pen on the table in an annoying staccato rhythm.

"What's up, Abe? I've never seen you this nervous."

"My Jewish upbringing, I guess. I've never dealt with nuns before. You're Catholic, Jim. How're you handling this?"

The investigator sorts through a mishmash of feelings. Denial at first, he recalls. Then disappointment, followed by confusion, then anger. Words fall short.

"A nun therapist getting sexually involved with a client? How could she? It's not just about professional ethics. It's about a violation of her vow of celibacy and the morals the Church teaches..."

"Never did get that celibacy thing," Abe comments.

"What she did is so, so, so ..." he reaches for the right word, "... *hypocritical*. Wanna know what the nuns laid on us back in the day? Sex was THE BIG SIN. Even to think about it could land you in Hell. Tell that to a teenager," he pauses. "Took me a while to get past their ridiculous taboos."

"Really? That bad?"

"Oh, yeah. In my parochial school days what 'Sister said' carried a lot of weight. We thought the nuns just a little less than God. Oh, the innocence of youth." Jim shakes his head, puzzled at his own naiveté. "You know, those nuns still reside in my head, and in my heart. Part of me wants Carole to be wrong, but I know she's not."

He sighs, tosses his napkin on the table. "Did you know Carole wrote a letter to the mother superior, told her about Sister Amelia's sexual misconduct and the negative impact on her life? I saw the response she got."

Abe chooses not to interrupt his coworker. Sometimes it's important to just listen. That's what partners do.

"I haven't gotten over it yet, Abe. Mother Superior didn't offer an apology; she never even asked Carole what happened. Instead she wrote back: 'When you left the Order, you signed a paper that said you wouldn't hold us responsible for anything.' No compassion in that. She just lawyered up!"

"Really?"

"This from the Order Carole dedicated her life to for over ten years. Why they became like family when the teen left home. I saw what that betrayal did written all over Carole's face. She vowed she'd take this to the Archbishop, all the way to Rome if necessary. Then she sobbed, buried her head on the table for the longest time."

Jim stops to get control of his own emotions, then comments, "Her pain resonates in my own soul, Abe. I, too, feel betrayed by my Church. How could a nun, a representative of God, be that cold and defensive?"

Jim looks away. He never really intended to share his religious crisis with a coworker from another faith. Somehow it just slipped out.

"Here's some feedback, Jim. I hear you saying you don't want to believe it. Sound familiar?"

"Yep." Jim looks down sheepishly. "Guess I'm reacting just like those therapists did. They didn't want to believe it and I don't want to believe it either. That's why I wanted you to come along. You've gotta take the lead on this one, Abe."

"Speaking as the outsider here," Friedman answers. "When someone brings a stool into the therapy room three separate times, disrobes, and puts her breast in a patient's mouth, that's sexual, not maternal or therapeutic. That's clear as can be to me. I don't understand why Carole struggles with that."

"Maybe she just doesn't want to believe it either." Jim speculates. "Like me."

He ponders Abe's words before responding. "Nuns sometimes did weird things. When we were learning cursive writing, my second grade teacher wrapped our knuckles with a wooden ruler if we didn't stay in the lines. What kind of God would do that to little kids? We just didn't have fine motor control yet. Of course, you don't think way that when you're a little kid. You just accept it, and blame yourself."

There's silence for awhile as the two men wrap their heads around the nun's strange behavior. Friedman is taking a seminar that focuses on unethical medical practices. In class they discussed the behavior of a transactional analysis therapist Jacqui Lee Schiff, who engaged in an extreme brand of reparenting.

"Schiff actually put her patients in diapers, bottle fed them, made them call her mom, spanked them, bathed them," he says. "It wasn't until a patient at her institute died from scalding while being bathed, that authorities eventually investigated what was going on at her place. One patient testified she had seen a patient nurse at Schiff's breast though there was no milk coming."

"Jesus Christ! That's just fucking nuts!" Jim throws his hat into the air. "Are you suggesting Sister Amelia bought into that?"

"I just don't know. Schiff got a lot of attention: a book, talk shows, awards—though she was eventually ousted from the profession. My point: we need to monitor rogue mental health workers like Schiff and Amelia. Some do pretty weird things in the name of therapy."

"Guess we'll know more after we talk to her," Jim suggests.

"No matter what our feelings about Amelia, we have to be careful how we approach her, Jim. We can't afford to alienate a critical witness in our case against Jansen. Much as I hate, we may end up doing some plea bargaining here."

"I hate it when people who don't deserve leniency get it!" Jim grumbles.

# 38

The two men pull into the campus parking lot a few minutes early. Abe inhales deeply as they make their way across a carefully manicured lawn to the main building. "Here goes," he says, adjusting to his full height as he opens the front door.

An elderly nun receptionist checks their credentials at the front desk, alerts Sister Amelia of their arrival, and then escorts the two men to an office in the back of the building. As they walk down the long corridor Abe studies portraits of esteemed clergy from the past, stern-faced men in tri-cornered red birettas topped with puffy pom-poms.

He prefers the occasional Bible scenes that break up the monotony. Like the one of the kindly Shepherd cuddling a wounded sheep in his arms. And Jesus extending a helping hand to Peter who is about to sink in a stormy sea. That aspect of Catholicism appeals much more to his Jewish heart than the pomp of the Vatican.

The small visitor's room holds four wingback chairs grouped around a central coffee table. A lamp casts shadows on the scene of Jesus inviting children to come to Him. An otherwise bare wall holds a carved wooden crucifix, a universal symbol of the price one must pay for speaking truth to power.

A chunky, soft-spoken nun in her early sixties nervously awaits their arrival. Sister Amelia is dressed in a hybrid outfit: a modern just-below-the-knee navy blue skirt, topped by a plain long-sleeved white blouse accented with a gold cross on a chain. A short black veil holds an obvious wig in place. Abe senses the motherliness that Carole latched on to. He produces his credentials and introduces Jim as his investigative partner.

Friedman positions himself directly opposite Sister Amelia where he can observe her body language. "Thank you for agreeing to meet with us," he begins. "As I told you on the phone, we're here to talk about the Carole Thornton case."

"Yes," Sister Amelia replies. "Yes. I've been so troubled about Carole. I should never have referred her to Dr. Jansen," the nun confesses, wringing a hanky as she speaks. "I was new to my profession, so inexperienced . . . on my own, so isolated from other professionals in my field."

She searches his face for understanding.

Finding none, she continues a little less sure of herself. "I scarcely knew the man. A physician, a volunteer at our Health Center introduced me to Dr. Jansen, a Catholic psychiatrist about to open his own private practice downtown. Jansen was Catholic, and available. It seemed like an answer to my prayers."

Jim just cannot contain his irritation. The nun's excuses are not sitting well with him. "She spent her adolescence in your order with no exposure to men. She was out on her own for the first time. To me what you did could be compared to declawing a cat and then sending it out to fend for itself."

He gets a dirty look from Abe, and decides he'd better shut up.

Sister Amelia attempts a different strategy. "Let me explain the situation back in the early sixties, Jim, so you can understand." She clears her throat to tell her story. "I encouraged Carole to share an apartment with Jeanne, a former nun and former patient of mine who also needed a place to live. Jeanne was pregnant at the time, but she hadn't told either of us. She overdosed while Carole was at school. When Carole came home, she found Jeanne unconscious just shortly before the police arrived on the scene. Luckily, Jeanne had notified her psychiatrist who called the authorities. The police were none too friendly to Carole. Acted as if it was somehow her fault. That whole experience scared her—scared me, too."

Sister Amelia's eyes plead for understanding, maybe even absolution. She gets only silence, so she continues to recall the sequence of events.

"I lost confidence in myself. I didn't want a second suicide on my hands. I told myself a male therapist might do a better job helping Carole to adjust to the world than I could. She didn't want to switch to Dr. Jansen, but I pushed her into it." Sister Amelia wipes her forehead with her man-size hanky. Suddenly she's locked in a coughing fit.

"I need something," the nun explains as she gets up from her chair. "My mouth is very dry. Would you like coffee or tea?" Both men decline.

The goal, Abe reminds Jim while she's out of the room, is cooperation, not judgment or intimidation.

Upon her return with a cup of tea, Sister Amelia picks up her narration. "After Jeanne's suicide attempt, I asked the physician who volunteered at our medical center to prescribe something for Carole as a stop gap measure. He prescribed some rather powerful drugs. Sparine and Elavil, if I remember correctly. The follow-up therapy was to be with Dr. Jansen."

In spite of himself, Jim breaks in. "Let's cut the crap and get to the nitty-gritty. Did you maintain any contact with Carole?" Anderson asks, determined to get the information he needs.

The nun reports getting a wedding invitation a couple of years after losing touch with Carole. She sent a card, but did not attend the event

"So how did you two connect after that?" Anderson asks.

"Several years into her marriage, I got a call from her. She asked to see me professionally. I agreed."

She pauses to sip her tea before continuing. "When patients contact a therapist after a long absence, usually something's going wrong in their lives. I could hardly say no. So we resumed weekly therapy for awhile."

Friedman interrupts. " Did she pay you?"

The nun answers in the negative. Since Carole was a former patient and a former member of the Order in need of help, there was never money involved. Abe wraps his legal mind around this unusual situation. Money is typically used to establish a relationship as professional; but then, clerical counseling rarely involves the exchange of money. He decides to leave that for the Psychology Board attorney to unravel.

The nun continues the narrative. "When Carole came for our first appointment, she brought a plaque along. It read 'O Great Spirit, let me never judge my neighbor until I have walked one moon in his moccasins.' She always had a great love for Native American culture."

"I was touched by the immense sorrow on Carole's face that day. She knelt on the floor in front of me—in a blue skirt and white blouse, typical of the uniforms Catholic School students often wear. She wanted me to understand, to forgive her. She was, in that moment, a Prodigal Daughter coming home totally broken in spirit. While I held her in my arms, she told me Dr. Jansen had sexualized his therapy. She said she finally managed to escape his hold on her when she met Arvid, the man she eventually married."

Jim Anderson stares out the window, struggling to contain his fury, not sure if he can bear to hear any more. Friedman remains steady in his resolve to uncover the facts of the case. He clears his throat, adjusts his gaze until he looks deeply into the nun's deep blue eyes.

"I have to ask you this. Carole claims in a letter she sent to the Psychology Board that you also engaged in intimate sexual behavior with her while she was under your care. Is that true?"

Sister Amelia is prepared to answer. When first contacted by the Psychology Board, she immediately reported the letter to her superiors who then contacted their attorney. He recommended cooperation in the investigation. He suggested that would protect the Order from the least amount of negative publicity. So her superiors ordered the nun to cooperate and do her best to clean up the mess.

The nun admits to her malpractice. "We all know what I did," she mutters. "It was in the letter she wrote."

Abe and Jim glance at each other in mild astonishment. Sexual predators don't often confess so readily to their misconduct.

"You do know this could cost you your license, don't you?" Friedman warns.

The nun nods. She never wanted to be a psychologist in the first place. When her superiors ordered her to train in the field, she did so in the spirit of her vow of obedience. It was never easy; her studies left her in constant conflict with convent practices of the time.

She places her empty tea cup down on the lamp stand. "Religious life was destroying me as well as her. That's why I advised Carole to leave. I never had the guts to leave myself. I should have long ago, but too late now. I've invested most of my life here."

The two men squirm in their seats. Neither buy her attempt to play the victim in all of this.

"Guess maybe you needed a therapist as much as Carole did," Anderson mumbles, too soft for her to hear.

"Losing my reputation will hurt more than losing my license." She pauses, pulls nervously at a gray hair that has slipped out of place, then tucks it back under her pill box veil.

Wanting to relieve the mounting tension in the room, Friedman assures her that the Psychology Board would take her remorse into consideration. As his sense of judicial fair play kicks in, he puts up his hands to signal her to back off. "I won't be dealing with your misconduct, just Dr. Jansen's. You need to follow your attorney's advice. Pretty sure he wouldn't want you to say anything more about it."

When he stands up to leave, Anderson follows suit. "Thank you for your time. I'll get back to you soon."

Sister Amelia weakly raises her hand in a farewell gesture. As the door closes, she begins to sob at the prospect of what lies ahead for her.

"Shit!" Jim exclaims as he's almost side-swiped while merging on to rush hour traffic on the freeway. "Never saw him coming. Guess I'd better focus on the road."

As they reach the countryside, where traffic begins to thin out, Jim begins to process their interview with Sister Amelia out loud. "That was the best acting I've seen in years," he says. "You both deserve an Oscar: she for best actress and you for best supporting actor!"

"No apologies, smart guy," Abe responds. "I did what I had to do. We need her testimony for the Jansen case. You put that in jeopardy with your stupid remarks."

Jim defends his behavior by pointing out the nun was appealing for sympathy, and that was one game he was not going to get sucked into even if she came across sweet, compassionate, and maternal.

"The order was Carole's family for ten years," he says. "I saw a ton of hurt and betrayal, a deep love/hate relationship in Carole's eyes. That's something that's best settled around the kitchen table, not in a courtroom. Our job is to protect the public from future abuse."

At that moment, a frightened doe runs across the highway. Jim slows down to avoid hitting it. He pauses to regain his equilibrium before continuing. "I don't see how that's going to happen if the Psychology Board lets her trade her testimony for leniency. Who's she going to abuse next?"

Abe reminds his partner that Sister Amelia could have denied all of this. If she had, they'd probably have buried Carole's file, labeled her a mental case with a wild imagination. Sexual intimacy with two separate therapists? One a doctor, one a nun? Who would've believed that?

"I'm an investigator, trained to look for clues," Jim replies. "There's a big red herring in the picture, Abe. That stool the nun brought into the room for the purpose of nursing her. Sister Amelia's behavior was premeditated. She did it three times and might have continued if Carole hadn't called her on it. That's one place the two of them differ in their story. The nun says she did it once, perhaps a slip in an emotional session. Carole reports it happened three times. I tend to believe Carole."

The two men are silent for miles as they wrap their heads around the evidence gathered today. Sister Amelia will corroborate Carole's testimony, if the nun doesn't lawyer up and change her story. She will provide clear and convincing evidence the sexual activity actually occurred.

Traffic picks up as they approach the state capital. It's been a long day, leaving them with lots to ponder, including the question of why this abuse happens in the first place. Jim raises that issue. "I always assumed people went into the helping professions with the best of intentions. What happens along the way to change them?"

Abe comes up with some possible explanation: burnout from listening to the problems of the world, turning to drugs or alcohol for escape, becoming addicted to work, and forgetting to take time to care for themselves.

Jim throws in something he's been pondering. "Therapists aren't gods. They're human. Are they blind to their own weaknesses? They have issues, too, just like the rest of us."

Upon entering the city, Jim hears the chiming of the evening Angelus. It evokes memories of his Catholic upbringing, with its centuries-old monastic practice of turning to God in prayer three times a day. "What do you suppose happened to Carole's faith in all of this?"

Abe asks, "Which faith? Faith in God or faith in humanity?"

"Aren't they kind of linked?" Jim responds.

"Ah, Jim the philosopher. That's a side of you I don't often see."

"There's a lot about me you don't know," Jim grumbles as he parks the government vehicle on the now mostly empty state lot.

Abe gathers his papers from the back seat. "I'm just glad I have a wife and kids to go home to tonight. I plan to forget about this case until Monday. So, Jim, what are your plans for the evening? A date? Meeting a friend at the bar? Got something to bring you out of this darkness?"

"Naw, just another night in front of the boob tube."

"How about coming home with me for supper? There's life outside of the office. Don't you ever forget that."

# 39

News from the hospital shatters Carole's day. Her dad will remain in the ICU indefinitely, with no guarantee of recovery. It's difficult to communicate with him. Periodically, he regains consciousness, but he can't talk because of the tracheotomy and he's too weak to write.

That leaves family members wondering what his look of discontent means. Her sister suggests he wants to die. He's asking someone to pull the plug.

Carole frowns. Not true. Dad is not a quitter. He beat pancreatic cancer five years ago. He'll lick this cancer, too, she tells herself.

As she looks at the man growing weaker by the day, she remembers all he has been in her life. Little things come to mind: how he slowed down when her small legs struggled to keep up as they trudged to the local library . . . how he taught her about the constellations in the classroom of the skies on a warm summer night . . . how he named trees and animals as they walked through the forest and along the lake shore . . . how he took her to a Harlem Globetrotters game. He has been her role model: lector and usher at Church, caretaker for the poor in the parish, president of the men's Holy Name Society. She learned so much about life from him.

She wonders if her lawsuit might be the cause of his current struggle to communicate. They never discussed it. There's little time left to do so now. When the others leave and she's alone with him, she raises the issue. She explains, "The lawsuit. It's something I have to do."

He shakes his head. Hard to interpret that. He looks away, as frustrated as she is with their inability to communicate.

Carole adds, with tears in her eyes, "I'm your daughter. I'm not a quitter either. This is something I just have to do."

A specialist drops in with a new treatment plan—some experimental drug. He writes a prescription but dispenses little hope.

The room is quiet tonight save for the beep, beep, beep of a life-monitoring machine and the whoosh, whoosh of oxygen, mechanically-delivered to her dad's faltering lungs. Being long past visiting hours, auxiliary staff and physicians no longer crowd around the nursing station inserting their presence into the death watch with their low-key conversations.

When Carole finally leaves, she rides an empty elevator to the lobby. Tonight it doesn't transport newly-birthed grandparents who carry flowers and balloons in celebration of a new life.

She exits through the glass door into a barren parking structure. By now, late-night movie patrons have left the neighborhood theatre and even the bar traffic has thinned. The deserted city streets only add to her loneliness. Even the stars bed themselves behind impenetrable clouds.

It takes three more months for Carole's dad to die. His leg is the next part of him to give out. It turns a telltale black as gangrene sets in. The grandkids whisper among themselves, curious about what that means. Carole overhears her mother whisper, "It's okay. You can let go. We'll be all right."

Once home, Carole falls into bed, way too exhausted for pillow talk, but there are things Arvid insists they must discuss—tonight. He clears his throat. That signals trouble.

"Can't it wait until morning?" Carole pleads. "I'm already on overload."

He explains that he has to make an important decision tomorrow that will affect the whole family. The tension in Arvid's voice cuts through her exhaustion. She rolls over to face him and notices there are tears in his eyes.

"I lost my job," he whispers.

Carole jolts into full alert.

"What? How? Why?"

"A few months ago . . . a few months ago," he stutters, ashamed of what he did. "Umm, this kid . . . he always mouths off, wouldn't listen . . . his mom always defends him . . . he finally got to me. I grabbed his shirt and pinned him up against the wall. That's all. He complained to his mom. She called the principal."

Carole's been taught you don't kick a man when he's down. She doesn't. Seeing his remorse, she chooses instead to mask her terror at losing their economic security to slip into problem-solving mode.

"Can you go to the union?" Carole suggests.

"I did. They fought for my job for months. It's a Board decision. They said I can finish up the school year but they will not renew my contract. They want me to leave teaching and said they won't challenge unemployment compensation if I do that. That's all the union has been able to negotiate for me."

"UC—that part is good," she comments, trying to think of something positive to say. "It'll put food on the table."

Arvid shares the plans he has already put in place. He describes a new high-tech retraining program he qualifies for under the Job Training Partnership Act. Admission to the intensive study requires a bachelor's degree; he has a master's. In one year, participants will earn an associate degree. He's already been accepted.

"The program recruiter at the Tech School said I have the highest mechanical reasoning score he's ever seen," he adds in an attempt to preserve a miniscule token of dignity.

He shares that he has already applied for a job doing inventory work on the week-ends. It will require him to get up in the middle of the night but he'll manage. The job starts as soon as the school year ends.

Impressed with his initiative, Carole searches for words of encouragement. "I've been through this before, Arvid. I left the convent with nothing but the clothes on my back and a hundred bucks in my pocket. I made it then and we'll make it now." She doesn't add there are five of them to provide for now.

Carole reminds Arvid that she's made some important connections through her volunteer work. When she gets her master's degree in May, she'll be looking for a job. "If I can't find a job, then I shouldn't be volunteering at a career center teaching other people how to do it," she adds.

Arvid apologizes for not telling her about his situation sooner. "You were going through so much. I didn't want to add to your troubles."

"We'll work this out," she says. "I know we will. Now let's get some sleep so we can deal with tomorrow," she suggests.

Sleep eludes her. Her mind whirls searching for any positives in what just happened. . . Arvid will get away from the teacher who thinks it's cool to tease the only male teacher in the elementary school by putting seductive pictures on his desk. . . He won't have to listen to snide remarks of male relatives who call him 'a school marm'. He's very good at fixing things, he learned that on the farm and in the Army; he might be happier using those skills. . . The kids at his school will be losing a fine science teacher and a dedicated softball coach. Their loss, she concludes.

# *40*

The next morning, Carole is left alone in an empty house, while Arvid signs the agreement that will end his career as an educator, and place the family in serious financial straits. She thinks of all the sacrifices they made, the time and tuition they spent to put him through graduate school—now all wasted.

The blame game begins in her inner world, as it does so often when one is exhausted. A venomous voice suggests Arvid might be better off without her. She just drags him down. Without her they would have a better chance at future happiness, the voice suggests. The family might be sad at first but without her he could move on, find a better mother for the kids, one that isn't chronically mentally ill.

She tries to concentrate on a resume, but finds it impossible to identify any positive accomplishments when that voice keeps telling her what a failure she is.

"I'll get to it tomorrow," she sighs, and turns to housework instead.

When yesterday's tomorrow arrives, she picks up the same blank sheet to list the things she does well. The same negative voice interrupts. It reminds Carole her Dad won't be around much longer. There'll be no support coming from him.

"You disappointed him, you know," the voice scolds.

"I tried to make him proud of me."

"Well, you sure failed, didn't you."

Carole puts the tear-stained paper aside. Who'd want to hire her? Anyway, it's time to pick up the kids.

The following day, the volume of that nagging voice grows exponentially. "Three strikes and you're out, lady."

"What are you, some kind of umpire?" she snaps back.

"Strike one: the convent."

"It was hard stuff," she explains. "Kneeling on a stone floor before a council of superiors just to beg for admission. Kissing the floor and begging pardon for dropping a fork in the refectory during spiritual reading. Getting up at 2 A.M. to pray in chapel for the sinners of the world who were out on the town. Bad enough but it was that last year of total seclusion, away from everything and everyone important to me, that did me in. When they put us under a gigantic pall during the Profession ceremony and declared us dead, I was already dead inside."

"So you quit."

"I tried," she defends. "By then, I had begun to doubt the existence of their God. I turned for help."

"Boy, you picked a pretty screwed-up therapist to help you. You didn't even have the sense to walk away from her, did you?"

"She was the only one available to me in the convent."

Carole leaves the kitchen table and heads to the medicine cabinet to retrieve an antidepressant before tackling that elusive resume.

"Strike two: your marriage," the voice continues. "Not working out so well either, is it?"

"We tried marriage counselors, marriage enrichment classes, family therapy," she argues. "What more could we do?"

"Ah. Strike three: motherhood."

"Shut up! I love my kids. I take them to the library, to the swimming pool, for walks in the park, for picnics. I select the best schools for them. I help them with their homework. I volunteer at Cub Scouts and teach CCD on Saturday."

She grows sad as she admits she's not always sure what she should do. She reads Dr. Spock, but she feels very insecure about parenting. She doesn't want her kids to turn out like her. She gets up, tosses another tear-stained sheet in the basket, and sets a clean one in front of her.

"Shut up! Enough. I'll never get this resume written."

Besieged by guilt and shame, Carole's resistance is now totally depleted. She rips the Wonder Woman pendant from her neck and tosses it on the floor.

The voice jeers at her. "About time you got rid of that silly thing. You're no Wonder Woman. You're just a wondrous failure, an F-minus in teacher terms."

Carole is desperate for reinforcements in this ongoing attack. Her therapist. Chemicals. God.

She dials Dr. Schubachs's number and gets an answering machine. She crosses that one off the list and goes to the next one.

She scribbles an apology to Arvid for the darkness she has brought into his life—the anxiety, the anger, the mounting hospital bills. She encourages him to find a better wife and a better mother for her children.

Then she fills a paper bag with every pain relieving chemical in the medicine cabinet: antidepressants, anti-anxiety drugs, antihistamines, antibiotics—anything stored in a medicine bottle, even throws cough syrups into the stockpile.

There is one last thing she needs to do. She must make her peace with God if she is going to do this. Churches aren't generally open at this hour, but the chapel a scant mile away might be. She gets into her Mercury Comet, sets the paper sack on the front seat, and drives away.

As she slips into the back pew of the chapel, she recognizes the nuns are singing Compline, the final prayer in the Divine Office, the one that marks the end of a monastic day.

"No greater love than this, to lay down one's life for a friend," the voice counsels her. "That's what Jesus said. And that's what he did."

Suddenly peace flows into her tormented soul. Her life for theirs. Soon she will see her God. She's now sure He is okay with what she plans to do.

"You're doing the right thing," the voice assures her. "Things will be better when you're out of the picture."

Carole returns to her car where she consumes everything in the paper bag. She begins humming a spiritual. "Soon very soon, we're going to see the King."

Her breathing eventually grows shallow as the sun slips below the horizon. In the darkness that follows, she whispers a final prayer for her family before slipping into unconsciousness.

As the sun rises, Carole stirs. In the front seat of her car, groggy and confused, but certainly not in Paradise. A voice in a tunnel of light ordered her return. "Go back. You must finish the work you have begun."

To do that she needs help. Soon. Or it might be too late.

Carole turns the key still dangling in the starter and heads home on streets devoid of traffic at this early hour. She scrapes a fire hydrant turning into the driveway permanently impressing evidence of her erratic driving on the passenger door.

The kitchen door opens. Arvid stands there with a stricken expression on his face that gradually changes to hope. He springs into action as she blacks out. Carole recalls nothing of what happened between arriving home and waking up in a hospital bed at suppertime.

Very few things that happen in the next few days leave a lasting impression on her. She recalls that her teenage niece Linda who works in dietary sent up a second strawberry shortcake on her supper tray. She cried at that sweet touch.

She remembers how when her chemical-laden body resisted sleep the second night on the ward, a psych nurse sat by her bedside, using relaxation techniques and a warmed blanket to relieve her patient's insomnia.

Small kindnesses, but still quite effective in reviving her fighting spirit. Slowly, her wounded psyche heals.

# 41

Soon the hospital discharges her to resume life as usual. Newly rested and energized, she completes her resume and turns her attention back to completing her graduate studies.

Reviewing the game plan developed in her Leadership for Change class, she must do some serious consciousness-raising about sexual abuse by therapists.

With her two lawsuits, she has already engaged regulatory and criminal law enforcement. She has addressed politicians by testifying at a public hearing and through ongoing correspondence with the governor's advisor on women's issues. She's been invited to train mental health workers on abuse of power issues, and has done so willingly. She's encouraged the local Mental Health Association to form a survivor support group.

She believes her own case could help inform the public if she catches the attention of the media. She values its influence in the court of public opinion, but how can she engage them? Her thoughts are interrupted by an incoming phone call.

"Hello, this is Chris Tardio with Oprah Winfrey at *A.M. Chicago*. Am I speaking to Carole Thornton?"

She sighs, one of those silly crank calls, but resists the urge to hang up. "Yes, this is Carole," she replies. How did this person get her number? Who the heck is Oprah Winfrey anyway? Probably a survey or a plea for donations, she surmises. If they only knew her current financial status they wouldn't be bothering her. She waits for the predictable pitch.

"We plan to do a TV show on sexual abuse by therapists. Your case has been brought to our attention. Would you consider coming to Chicago as a guest presenter for our Friday broadcast?"

"M—m—me?" Carole stutters. "Why me? How'd you get my name?"

"We have our ways," Tardio responds.

Carole's mind spins. TV? Chicago? How?

"Psychologist George Marquardt will be our featured expert," Tardio says. "We're looking for a couple of women to talk about their personal experience. George suggested you."

Carole knows about Marquardt. He's a leading expert on the national effort to end abuse. How does he know about her?

Tardio explains that *A.M. Chicago* is more than a local show: it's carried by its affiliates across the nation as well.

Carole decides it's best not to tell Tardio she doesn't know who

Oprah is or much about her show or that she's just not into day-time TV.

She weighs what that opportunity offers. A chance to meet Marquardt. A chance to reach a whole lot of people, including fellow survivors. On the flip side, Carole shudders at the loss of privacy. People, maybe even relatives, will see her as a mental patient. What will her neighbors think? Will she lose friends?

"You seem hesitant," Tardio notes.

Suddenly she remembers the voice that ordered, "Go back and finish the work you have begun." This is now the purpose of her life. She'll have to face her fears. She will speak out for those victims who cannot yet speak for themselves.

Tardio explains that Oprah will ask questions and she will just have to answer her. That's something Carole can handle. She agrees to come. Tardio then fills her in on the arrangements. An airplane ticket will arrive express later today. Carole cringes. She's never flown in an airplane before. That will be a first.

The producer wants Carole to come the day before, stay in a hotel at their expense, and have an evening meal with the other guests "to get to know them better." A driver will pick her up at the airport, drive her to the hotel, and take her to the studio in the morning several hours before show time. "Oprah likes to talk to her guests before the show," Tardio explains.

After she hangs up, Carole collapses in a chair. "Whew. Wait 'til I tell Arvid and the kids," she says to the cat who rubs her leg affectionately. "I'm going to be on Oprah." He couldn't care less; all he wants is food.

Jack, always first home from school, skips around the living room when Carole breaks the news. "Can I tape it, Mom? Can I?"

When his brothers arrive, he's waiting at the front door to broadcast the news. "Mom's gonna be on Oprah. Mom's gonna be on Oprah!"

Their faces drop. Their Mom? On Oprah? Really? "Oh, sure," they mutter dubiously.

But their mother's face says it's true. Carole grins. She's suddenly a celebrity in her own home.

"Mom's going to Chicago," they shout in unison when Arvid arrives much later. "She's going to be on Oprah Winfrey's show."

"Really?" He stares at his wife in disbelief.

That night Carole dreams she is transported by a jet plane to the tarmac in Oz, landing there with a gentle thud, thud, thud. Fellow passengers disembark and swarm around Glenda the Good Witch of the North, who holds up a sign with Carole's name on it. Glenda says the Wizard is waiting. Just as Carole opens her mouth to protest, she feels the sharp snap of Glenda's wand on her arm.

Jack, her real life munchkin, needs his lunch money. That brings her swiftly home to Kansas. As she vacates a surreal Oz, she wonders where this yellow brick road will lead and who will companion her along the way?

# 42

Arvid knows better than to oppose his wife when she's made up her mind to do something, so he goes with the flow. He anticipates nervous energy will fuel Carole safely through her first airplane ride. He drives her to the airport, waves good-bye at the gate and prays that all will go well for his wife. Perhaps the tide is turning at last. Something positive for a change.

Treading on unfamiliar ground, Carole decides to follow the lead of other more experienced travelers. She finds her seat and buckles in place. When the plane reaches cruising altitude, her thoughts drift. The faces of the victims she has met float by in the clouds outside the window, each with a story to tell.

In what seems no time at all, the pilot announces, "Prepare for landing." Passengers disembark like worker bees intent on a swift departure from the hive. Carole follows. With two feet back on solid ground, she gives herself a psychological pat on the back. She's survived her first plane ride. She has no difficulty locating her ride in the O'Hare terminal. A uniformed driver displays a large sign with her name on it, just as Tardio said he would.

"Miss," he offers, "may I carry your bag?" Courteous but professionally distant, the driver escorts her to a limo parked at the curb, and opens the rear door for her.

She wonders does the driver know she's not a big celebrity? She's just a homemaker whose kids shrieked with excitement when they learned their Mom was going to be on TV. She luxuriates in her first-ever limousine ride, but grows more anxious when she realizes she doesn't know the proper protocol. Is a tip required? If so, how much? Or does the TV show take care of that detail? She opts to give him one. He doesn't refuse.

The driver escorts her to the concierge for check-in. After giving final instructions for the morning pick-up, he departs, and a bellhop escorts Carole to her room. She gasps at the accommodations. She gazes out the window at the Chicago streets, bustling with pedestrians and bumper-to-bumper traffic. In the distance, she sees Lake Michigan waters painted many colors by the bluster of the Windy City. In the bathroom, she buries her face in the softest towels she has ever touched, and smells the perfumed soaps. Then she flops on the queen-sized bed she will have all to herself.

The phone intrudes on her nap. A caller identifies himself as George Marquardt. He invites Carole to join him and another guest in the hotel restaurant at 7 P.M.

"Sure," she stammers. "Seven is fine." Who wouldn't want dinner with him?

George welcomes her to the table, not as a lesser but as a fellow presenter. The onus of being a mental patient slips away. Unfamiliar with the proper protocol for fine dining, Carole follows George's lead while ordering.

"The show will pick up the cost so we might as well enjoy the best," he coaches. "I'm hungry for a good steak. What tempts you?"

Carole selects filet mignon while Joan, the other guest, orders North Atlantic salmon.

As appetizers are served, George initiates a conversation about the upcoming show. "I've read about your case," he tells Carole. "I am so pleased to hear what you are doing."

"To be honest, I'm surprised you even know about my case," Carole responds. "I read about you while I was doing library research at the university. I'm thrilled to finally meet you." Then she turns her attention to Joan. "Where are you from?"

"I'm from the Chicago area."

"A Midwesterner, like George," Carole notes. "I must admit, my vision has been pretty narrow. I'm not up on what's happening in other states."

George informs them of a survivor network slowly building across the nation. He offers to give them contact information for consumer groups currently active in Seattle, New York, and Texas.

"That would be so helpful, Dr. Marquardt," Carole says.

"Please, call me George."

"Um, George . . . how did you ever get to be the expert in this area?" Joan inquires.

George explains how that grew out of his work at the Drop-In Counseling Center in Detroit, which provides mental health services to people regardless of their ability to pay. An alarming number of patients reported sex with a previous therapist. The staff decided they needed to do something about that abuse. He took the lead.

"But it never happens," Carole interjects, in a voice thick with sarcasm. "Patients only imagine it!"

"We never assume patients are lying or imagining it," George assures her. "We've been collecting hard data for years. I'll discuss our findings on the show."

Carole asks, "Will you talk about the trauma that follows?"

"Certainly. But on that score your voices will be more powerful than mine. I commend you both for speaking out."

"You never know how the audience will react," Joan sighs wistfully. "I sure hope they'll get it."

"Some will, some won't," George says. "But the message will go out beyond the studio. WGN has an extensive national outreach. Oprah is a well-respected talk show host. I hear she's about to go national with her own show in a few months."

Conversation and a second glass of wine mellows Carole's anxiety enough that she sleeps well beneath a downy comforter in the sound-deadened silence of her hotel room. She no longer feels so alone.

George and Joan are in the green room enjoying a continental breakfast when Carole arrives at the studio the next morning. All three spend time with make-up artists who prepare them for the camera.

Like a Chicago Bears quarterback, Oprah drops in to huddle with her team. After outlining her finely-tuned game plan, she leaves. The producer then stops by with particulars.

"While in the green room, you'll be able to watch what's happening on that monitor in the corner of the room," she points out. "I'll signal when it's your time to go on stage. George goes first. Carole, you go on after the first commercial break. Joan, after the second."

Though the monitor is on during the first part of the program, Carole is so focused on her own role, she scarcely hears what George says. At the producer's signal she moves quickly to the stage. She takes a seat next to Oprah wondering how in God's name she ever made it from a mental hospital to national TV. Bright lights temporarily blind her. Her heart is racing. Her tongue cleaves to the roof of her mouth. Then Oprah reaches out and places her hand on Carole's arm. Terror fades.

She focuses on the questions Oprah asks. She imagines speaking not to the sea of faces in front of her but to the victims in the audience who need to know, "You are not alone."

Carole meets two of those women after the show. One, who introduces herself as Christine, shares her story. More than two decades ago she was drugged, raped, and impregnated by her therapist. She reported him to authorities, but in the recommended cover-up, she put her child up for adoption. Today, she is a birth mother making serious headway in her search for the child of her womb, who is now coming into adulthood. She has seen him at a distance, but has not yet had the courage to approach him. She doesn't know how to explain his conception.

Christine introduces a much younger woman who accompanies her. Patty Ann reports a long history of psychiatric hospitalizations. During one stay, she was lured into a sexual relationship with her therapist. She was too young to know what to do about it. She had a history of schizophrenia, so who would have believed her anyway? But that seduction still haunts her.

When Oprah announced the topic of the day's presentation, both came hoping to connect with other survivors of therapist abuse. All three share a commitment to educate the public and mental health workers. They agree to help plan a conference after Carole's hearing is over. They hug, share contact information, and a promise to keep in touch.

Carole's appearance on *A.M. Chicago* kickstarts her role as a public media advocate. She carries her message to talk shows in Baltimore, Philadelphia, Detroit, Minneapolis, St. Louis and her own hometown. Connecting with survivors motivates her to continue, but the task isn't always easy. As George warned, "some in the audience will get it; some will not."

After she and a panel of survivors bare their souls to an audience at the *Sally Jessy Raphael* show, a woman in the back row stands up and says, "All you women got what you deserved." Carole cringes, in pain not for herself, but for the woman who understands so little about the abuse of power.

# *43*

Cognizant that the many legal delays are taking a serious toll on her family, Carole feels compelled to write a letter to the state-appointed hearing examiner, Thomas Fitzgerald, begging him to please expedite the proceedings. Fitzgerald feels equally compelled to share the contents of her letter with the defense.

In her letter, she expressed frustration with events that have occurred to date. Why, she asked, has she been required to turn over all her medical records to a man who is currently being charged with the misuse of confidential information for his own gain? In light of spousal privilege, why has the defense been allowed to subpoena her husband? What would happen to public transparency if the defendant was allowed the closed hearing he is requesting? Wasn't the very purpose of her complaint to create public awareness of the sexual abuse of mental health patients?

She expresses gratitude that Fitzgerald ruled Leanne will not be excluded from the hearing, in spite of the defense's argument that the presence of the Director of the Sensitive Crimes Unit might imply criminal sexual assault.

When Tisch meets with his client to discuss the examiner's letter, he advises that any more delays on their part might alienate the hearing examiner, and they do need him on their side.

"Yeah, well it's my career, not his that's on the line," Jansen bellows. "I'll take whatever time I need. That bitch is not going to beat me."

"Then you're putting your own damn defense on the line. What do you want to do next?"

"Find me some expert who'll testify she's psychotic, she's hallucinating, or she's just plain vengeful. The drug she was on when she first came to see me can be prescribed for schizophrenia."

"But it's in the records," Ben reminds him. "You took her off it. You wrote she didn't need such a powerful drug. And you never diagnosed her as schizophrenic. Neither did anyone else."

"We could argue I was wrong," Jansen suggests.

Tisch sighs. He'll give his client what he wants. "I know a guy who'll give any psych eval you want—for the right price."

"Damn that bitch! She won't be happy until I'm in the poor house." Jansen slams his fist hard enough on the end table to knock his empty shot glass to the floor. The carpet keeps it from shattering into pieces. "I know who you mean, Ben. That guy with the mammoth ego. The one who's always in the paper . . . what's his name again? Kelly or Shelly or something? He'll say anything. Just pay the bastard. My career's on the line."

"OK, boss."

Tisch is sure he's not cut out to be a criminal defense attorney. He finds it professionally demeaning to defend a guilty client who's lying through his teeth. But he does what he's told. He puts in a call to the psychiatrist-for-hire, and leaves a message when Kelly doesn't pick up .

"He's probably in court right now. I'll let you know his price and availability when he returns my call." Tisch heads for the door intent on escaping Jansen's tiresome tirades. No such luck.

"Damn, why didn't she just come to me in the first place? I'd have paid her off. It would have cost less in the long run."

"Don't you get it yet?" Tisch shouts, spinning around to face him. "She's after something else. She's not in this for the money."

"Everyone has an Achilles heel," Jansen says. "Give me time. I'll find hers," he swears.

"I never went to law school to destroy people's lives," Ben mumbles as he slams the door behind him.

A cleaning lady moves aside quickly as he rushes past her down the hall. "Never can trust anyone who comes out of that office," she mutters to herself. "Best to just stay out of the way."

Ben is hardly back to the sanctuary of his own office when the phone jingles. It's Jansen.

"Got it, Ben. Carole's Achilles heel."

Jansen goes on to suggest that maybe they could find a way to drive a wedge between Carole and her current therapist. Maybe without Dr. Schubachs's support, she might drop the case.

"It isn't her lawsuit. It's the state's. And if that's what you plan to do, leave me out of it."

"You're my attorney!" Jansen barks. "You'll do what I tell you!".

"Don't use that tone of voice with me!" Ben snarls back. "I'm not your pawn!"

"I want you to find out everything you can about Carole's current therapist," the psychiatrist orders.

"Waste of money and manpower! Schubachs is highly respected. She's lily-clean, a professor at the Medical College, for God's sake. What could we possibly dig up on her?"

Jansen orders his attorney to hire a gumshoe just like the other side did. Eventually his attorney relents as his client pulls taut the leash of obligation and blackmail he always uses to shackle Ben.

"Get back to me when he turns in his report," Jansen adds.

Tisch slams the phone in its cradle. Jansen keeps digging the hole deeper and deeper. His client is lost in some crazy Wonderland of his own creation. If he insists on going down there, the ultimate judgment might very well be, "Off with his head!"

# 44

As the academic year draws to a close, it becomes more and more imperative for Carole to find employment. The family income will soon reach the poverty level. She needs to supplement Arvid's contribution until he finishes training. Now she must do for herself what she has taught other women to do.

She begins by putting out the word that she's looking for work. Mary, her mentor and colleague at the Women's Career Center, promises to keep her eyes and ears open. She delivers on that promise when she calls Carole's attention to a job posting that arrives in the mail.

"The Women's Center seeks a part-time career counselor to help clients find employment that will enable them to leave abusive relationships," Mary reads.

Being out of the workforce for a prolonged period of time leads women to undervalue their skills. Carole has seen that happen so many times. In her own knee-jerk response, Carole responds as she has seen so many do by dismissing it as out of reach. "I'm certainly not qualified."

"They're looking for someone with experience in advising women on career choice and job search. You've done that for months now. I'd give you a great recommendation. I'll bet your university advisor would too. Go for it, Carole."

Buoyed up by her cohort's enthusiasm, Carole reconsiders. "I do like that this position is part-time. Part-time is probably all I can handle right now."

"We'll miss you here, Carole, but I think you're ready to be launched."

It turns out the Women's Center is as interested in Carole as she is in them. The request for an interview comes within days of submitting her resume. Mary helps Carole role play the first job interview she's had in years.

Her mentor cautions, "An employer wants to know if you're qualified for the job. Focus on your skills and experience, not your personal life."

That advice calms the Carole's jitters about needing to account for the past two years she spent in psych hospitals. She'll be able to truthfully say she was acquiring a master's degree during that time. Still, she worries. Will she fit in after being out of the workplace so long? But she must move forward. The economic survival of her family depends on it. The stakes couldn't be higher.

The Women's Center is housed in an old Victorian home on the Upper East Side, in a pleasant quiet neighborhood within walking distance of the lake. As Carole steps into the parlor, a pudgy, friendly woman descends the stairs to welcome her.

"Hi, Carole, I'm Kathryn."

Recalling Mary's coaching, Carole takes her extended hand. It's the 1980's. Today's women must shake hands in business situations, just like men do, she reminds herself. She finds Kathryn's handshake firm and confident. She's afraid her own might be a bit sweaty.

"Do sit down," Kathryn invites when they enter her small office on the third floor, in an area of the house that might have once been sleeping quarters for some au pair in an earlier era. "Can I get you a cup of tea?"

"I'd love it," Carole responds, hoping the liquid will hydrate her dry mouth.

"I was thrilled that you applied for our new project," Kathryn begins. "I know a bit about your volunteer work with the Women's Career Center and with the Women's Crisis Line. We work together closely with the Crisis Line because abused women often call there for help."

Kathryn explains the project goals, concludes with a compelling fact. "Many women return to abusive situations. It's a price they pay for economic security. We want to stop that revolving door by helping them develop careers that pay a living wage. Would you be interested in doing that?"

"Very."

Carole senses an ally in this woman so she feels comfortable in explaining the transitions in her own life that might impact on her job: her father on his deathbed in the hospital ICU, her husband going through retraining after losing his job, child care responsibilities, and an upcoming administrative hearing she must attend. She explains her role as a primary witness in a case against a psychiatrist who sexually abused a patient. She cautions that the date has yet to be set so it could come at any time.

"Sorry to hear about your dad. And of course, you can take time off for the hearing. You'll be doing a favor for all women. How could we call ourselves the Women's Center if we didn't support you?"

Kathryn reaches into her desk for some forms. "It would be great if you could start next Monday. Let's get going on the paperwork to make this official.

Carole hopes Kathryn doesn't notice her struggle to hold back tears. She's overcome one giant hurdle. Now on to the next.

It's 9 P.M. on a typical Monday night at the tavern. Well-worn red vinyl bar stools are mostly vacant. While a bright light illuminates the idle pool table, the rest of the place is dark. The place reeks of smoke, stale beer, even of vomit and urine if one gets too close to the john. Without music blaring from the juke box or the characteristic display of aggressive male bravado, it's quiet—save for the monotonous voice of a TV sportscaster who lacks enthusiasm for his losing team.

An ill-shaven bartender leans against the wall, squinting as he attempts to read the evening paper in the meager light cast by an old black and white TV and a Hamm's sign touting the Land of Sky Blue Waters. A lone customer camps in a booth with his best buddy Jack Daniels for a companion.

Attorney Ben Tisch raises an eyebrow, wrinkles his nose as he enters. This is certainly not where he'd choose to meet. Reminds him of grubby places where the two of them hung out in their college days when they were first sowing their proverbial oats. Ben feels he's matured beyond this. Apparently his client has not.

As Tisch's eyes adjust to the dark, he spots his client in a far corner of the bar and approaches the booth.

"Hey, there, Ben," Jansen slurs.

"Guess you've been here awhile," Tisch sighs. Crap, another waste of his time, with little chance of any meaningful conversation when his client is in this condition

"Patients . . . cancelled. Every one of them. Thanks to the damn publicity." Jansen lifts a shot glass to slurp down his frustration.

Tisch ignores the whining. It's not like his client isn't getting exactly what he deserves. "We agreed to meet to share the PI's report," the attorney reminds him.

"So tell me, I'm listening," he claims as he pours another shot with an increasingly unsteady hand.

Tisch quickly grabs a napkin to wipe up the table before the overfill sullies the report. "Here's the scoop."

He reads directly from the PI report. Schubachs was once a nun, taught at the Mercy School of Nursing while in the convent.

"No, no, no. Not another nun! Three of 'em. How could I be soooo lucky?" He crosses himself.

The attorney continues to read. "She left the order, married, had two kids, resumed her education. Graduated from medical school where she specialized in psychiatry, was appointed to the faculty of the Medical College immediately thereafter."

"Her career's important," Jansen gripes, "doesn't care if she ruins mine . . . bitch."

"More important than you can imagine." Tisch reads on. "She's going through a nasty divorce, fighting for custody of the kids. Her ex claims she's an unfit mother, works such long hours that she's never around for the family. Neglect, he calls it."

"Heard that line before. My wife—my ex, I mean—Janine complained too—about my afterhours . . ."

Tisch refuses to open the door to Harry's past marital strife. They need to focus on the task at hand so he can go home to his wife and kids. He continues reading. "On the other hand, the husband hasn't had a job for over a year. He's a stay-at-home dad, not by choice but by circumstances. He claims the crazies his wife deals with pose a physical threat to the kids. He asked her to leave the County facility, but she refuses."

He shoves the report back in his briefcase. "That's all we got for now. The PI plans to keep digging. I will, too, when we subpoena her.

Personally I'm curious about how she got such a prestigious appoint-ment right out of medical school. That seems highly unusual."

"Wanna drink?" Jansen offers. "Bartender, bring me a glass," he calls.

That ticks Ben off. "Don't bother," he says, rising to leave. "Call me when you're sober enough to hear what I have to say," he adds as he starts to walk away—but can't. Something, someone pulls at his heartstrings. It would be easy to walk out on the drunkard in front of him, but he's also staring at the father of his godchild Lucy. Tisch can't bring himself to walk out on her. He sits back down, clears his throat.

"This place reminds me of bars we used to frequent in our youth, Harry," he says. "Back then, we bragged about our conquests, we compared notes on the girls we laid. Now we know—that wasn't really all that cool." He waits for his message to sink in. "We grew up, got married, and we both have daughters of our own."

"I love my little Lucy," Jansen drawls. "Doing this for her."

"I love her too," Tisch reminds him. "She's my godchild."

Is that tears he sees in his client's eyes? Maybe Tisch can reach him after all. "Imagine if one of Lucy's doctors had done to her what you did to Carole."

A dark sinister look passes over Jansen's face. "To my Lucy?"

Ben presses the point. "How would you feel? What would you do?"

Jansen's response is vehement. "I'd kill 'em."

Tisch pauses, giving Harry time to reflect a bit on what he just said. Then he delivers the punch line. "Don't forget Carole is some-one's daughter. So is Dr. Schubachs."

Jansen begins to sob. "I need my work. Lucy needs me."

"Lucy needs more than money from you, Harry. She just turned 13, still too young to fully understand what's going on but someday she will. Sooner than you think. How you going to explain the cover-up? What she really needs is a dad she can respect, a person who is man enough to admit his mistake, someone willing to make amends to people he's hurt. Give her that. It's worth more than money. It's not too late. Just do it, Harry."

"I can't, Ben. Just can't...I can't..." Jansen stares into nowhere land, wrapping his hand tightly around the neck of the whiskey bottle as if it could become a weapon of choice.

Tisch reads the signal, decides it's time to walk away. Jansen mumbles a bit incoherently. "Tell that PI, keep digging. You, too."

Tisch stops at the bar on his way out. "Hey, mister. Better call a cab. That guy's in no condition to be on the road."

He heads for his car. Crash, bang, clang. Tisch jumps. A shiver passes down his body. Just a raccoon prowling among the garbage cans. The attorney surveys the area carefully before unlocking his car. Seeing nothing of concern, he opens the back door and tosses his brief case on the car seat, next to his daughter's belongings.

"Cursed be the ties that bind us," he swears. "When will this ever end?"

The barkeeper puts down his newspaper and meanders over to Jansen. "No more drinks for you tonight," he says, confiscating the empty bottle. "Taxi'll be here soon."

Jansen drawls, "Wha'll I do with my Firebird?"

"Leave it on the lot. Pick it up by 2 tomorrow afternoon or I'll have it towed."

"I'm in deep shit," he whines, "really deep shit."


# 45

Dr. Schubachs, nervous about the upcoming deposition, accepts her brother's offer to act as her attorney. He advises his sister to draw from the expertise of previous psychiatrists who treated Carole. He suggests she invite them for a "forensic consultation," thereby waiving patient confidentiality.

Convinced that three heads would do better than one, she does as he advised. They accept her invitation.

The medical triumvirate meets in a remote windowless room, where there is little likelihood of being disturbed or overheard. As hostess and conveyor of the meeting, Schubachs serves her colleagues coffee—black and strong.

Oh, the ties that bind. These therapists have other things in common besides having treated Carole in the recent past. They've all had their records subpoenaed and are leery of having their psychiatric practices scrutinized by a state's attorney. Or even by fellow therapists, for that matter. They also hate testifying against a colleague. There's not a boatload of mutual trust in the room.

When Schubachs raises a discussion about Carole's diagnosis, the three begin to toss around their professional opinions like an old leather football at a Thanksgiving Day family get together. The two-minute warning has been called; the championship game is on the line. They need a Hail Mary pass to get through the hearing unscathed.

Dr. Orlanski is first to run with the ball. "It's the 1980's. Psychiatry is still a young science. Our methods are not yet well-defined. We can't take an x-ray of the psyche. We can't run a blood test before we select an appropriate treatment. We all had to diagnose her based on what we saw at the time. We had to label her for insurance purposes. We may have had different impressions. Let's begin by sharing our insights. I gather that's what this meeting is all about."

As the three compare notes, it becomes apparent that the diagnostic labels they assigned Carole were more a reflection of their own life experiences and worldview than any objective measurement. What they do concur on: fear of abandonment triggers most of Carole's "acting out."

Each recalls a time when she became suicidal after losing someone she depended on for emotional support. After comparing notes, Schubachs feels more confident. Abandonment does appear to be Carole's Achilles heel. There has been plenty of that in Carole's life, and Jansen was indeed one of culprits.

"Let's try to agree on a diagnosis so we don't look like a bunch of fools," Schubachs urges, "one that's in the latest DSM-III Diagnostic and Statistical Manual of Mental Disorders."

Dr. Mielke suggests they consider one of two diagnoses recently added to the 1980 edition. First, PTSD: posttraumatic stress disorder—maybe. They rule that out. It's currently associated with combat duty and she's had no military experience.

"Hmm, borderline might be appropriate," he suggests next, "though she fails to exhibit addictions usually associated with that diagnosis."

Professor Schubachs provides her own academic opinion. "Borderline is good. It's still a bit nebulous. It hasn't been thoroughly researched, nor is it widely understood. It's fast becoming the dumping ground for patients who are difficult to handle and she's certainly that. I think it would be fairly safe to stick with that diagnosis."

The three concur.

"I've never formally diagnosed her as depressed, but depression could also be present," Dr. Schubachs adds as an afterthought. Neither of the others disagree.

Schubachs can't resist challenging Orlanski about Carole's report that he once told her that it was inevitable she would commit suicide someday. She asks, "Didn't it occur to you that prediction might just heighten her anxiety when she was feeling suicidal?"

He offers no comment, excuse or apology. Instead he directs his anger at Jansen. "Can we all agree? Jansen ruined her life. For Pete's sake, what was he thinking? Guys like him give our profession a bad name."

Schubachs purses her lips, bites down hard to keep from chiding these two professionals. Neither did a thing when Carole reported sex with two previous therapists. She decides she'd better coach them on the upcoming legal process, or they'd probably screw that up, too.

Before Schubachs has a chance do that, Mielke throws in his two cents worth. "My money's on the defense playing dirty. Bet they'll hire Kelly to discredit anything you say. It's what the man does for a living. Talk about a disgrace to the profession…"

The chilling thought momentarily stops her cold. But Schubachs doesn't blink. So far she's been able to stand her ground with these men, so she's feeling ever more confident about holding her ground against Kelly, even though he's become an expert on court room strategies.

"One last thing," she says. "In order to revoke Jansen's license, Friedman needs to prove Jansen's misconduct poses a danger to the public safety."

"So it's about more than medical ethics?" Orlanski asks.

"I'm planning to testify that the sex instead of the therapy damaged Carole," Schubachs says. "She was young and could have been helped. She wasn't; in fact she was harmed by his dalliance. It's not just about ethics, it's about medical malpractice."

"Didn't Carole also report that a nun therapist engaged in some kind of sexual activity?" Mielke asks. "We never really discussed that much. I never brought it up. Guess I never thought it all that important. What about her?"

"Sister Amelia's admitted to what she did," Schubachs reports. "That's a plus. She'll testify that Carole reported Jansen's abuse to her very early on."

"What a sad, messy case," Mielke comments, stroking his Freudian beard. "An ugly portrait of our profession."

"Yes, it is." Schubachs gets up. "Well, thank you both for your input. I have to leave now. It's almost time for the deposition."

While waiting to testify, Dr. Schubachs paces nervously in her office. She inhales deep breaths to relieve her surging anxiety, then picks up the phone to put her brother on notice.

"It's time," she informs him. "They'll be arriving for the deposition in a half hour."

"I'm on my way."

He assures his sister that she'll do fine. She appreciates his vote of confidence. It bolsters her courage. She's following another piece of his advice. He suggested that the attorneys meet on his sister's turf. That reminds everyone that as a professor on the faculty of the Medical College, she holds a position that carries with it a certain prestige.

She waits to allow time for everyone to settle down in the conference room. Her brother had advised her to arrive last. "The CEO is usually last to arrive at company meetings, the judge is last to enter the courtroom, and the President of the United States arrives last when he delivers the State of the Union address," he'd pointed out. "It's another power play. You need all the power you can muster."

# *46*

Dr. Schubachs enters the conference room wearing a simple shirt-waist dress, casual shoes, rimless glasses, little make-up, and a serious but open expression. She hides her queasiness behind the shrewd and confident demeanor she developed as Mother Superior in her convent days, and continues to use to advantage when she finds herself in a tight situation.

The men rise as she takes her place at the head of the conference table. Introductions first. Then, at the court reporter's request, she raises her hand, swears to tell the truth, the whole truth, and nothing but the truth. "I do, so help me God," she murmurs rubbing her sweaty hands together under the table.

Testifying under oath is not new for the psychiatrist; she often provides the court with information it uses to determine placement for the mentally ill, homeless, and disenfranchised. What makes today different is that she's about to testify against a fellow psychiatrist who may be quite capable of challenging her expertise.

"Please spell your name slowly so I can get it in the records."

Jansen's attorney clarifies her credentials. When that's completed, he focuses on Dr. Schubachs' patient. The witness answers his questions in a curt, professional manner. No, Carole is not psychotic. Yes, she's honest. Yes, she suffers from her experience with Dr. Jansen. Yes, she recommended Carole do something about the past abuse. No, she did not suggest a law suit; that was Carole's idea. For most of an hour, Dr. Schubachs fields Tisch's questions as smoothly as she once fielded her State Boards.

While the legal ritual progresses, Schubachs subconsciously dissects Jansen inch by inch. The accused, slumped in his seat with his long legs extended, creates a facade of indifference. He refuses to meet her probing glances when she looks his way. She relaxes a bit. He is not as powerful as she imagined he would be. What she observes is his parasitic dependency on a relatively mediocre attorney.

Her stomach does a flip flop when the lawyer begins to inquire about her personal life. Dr. Bemmer's prophecy is coming true. *You will be on trial as much as Carole.*

"Were you once a nun?"

"Yes." How did they ever find that out? She rarely shares that with anyone.

"Were you not a member of the faculty of Mercy Hospital, one of the most feminist institutions in the country?"

"Yes." She holds her breath, anticipating his next question.

"Do you consider yourself a *feminist*?" Tisch asks in a tone that suggests that's a dirty word.

There was a time when Schubachs wore that label with great pride, but not since Medical School where it became a liability. Now under oath, she weighs how best to answer that question. After a slight hesitation, she responds, "Not especially." That makes her nervous. With a little digging, they could discover that's only a half truth.

"Don't you have a special interest in this case just because your professional goal is to practice in the clinic of the prominent feminist psychiatrist, Dr. Bemmer?"

"Not true." Could someone have seen them at the cafe, she wonders.

"Are you not in the midst of a divorce?"

She gulps. How much do they know anyway? "Yes."

"And isn't it true that your husband claims you're an unfit mother?"

His probing grows merciless, invasive. Her anxiety begins to soar.

Tisch studies the psychiatrist over the top of his glasses before posing a question that totally undercuts the scant equilibrium she retains. "Can you explain how you got such a prestigious position with the Medical College so soon after graduation? Isn't that a bit unusual?"

Schubachs pales, stiffens with indignation. "I don't see how that has any connection with this case, sir."

"So you're refusing to answer, then."

"Yes, for the reason I just gave you. I am not the one on trial here. Your client is."

She rises and calls for a break to consult with her attorney.

"You looked like a ghost in there," her attorney brother says once they reach the privacy of her office. "What's that all about?"

"What I have to tell you," she gulps, "is in confidence . . . client/attorney privilege, okay? You can't tell anyone . . . not even—especially not—the family . . . Promise?"

"Of course, Sis. What is it?"

"I . . ." she turns away before continuing. "I signed a nondisclosure settlement with the college."

"You did *what*?"

"One of the professors made a pass at me—threatened to flunk me if I didn't cooperate. I reported him to the head of the college."

He asks her how the administrator responded.

"Fully aware of the professor's reputation for womanizing, he offered me this position if I would just keep quiet. I signed a nondisclosure agreement and they gave me the job."

"Why didn't you come to me before signing that agreement?" her brother complains.

She stares at the floor. "I worked so hard to become a doctor. I couldn't risk losing my career. I shouldn't have agreed, but I did. I'm not proud of that. It's a secret I planned to carry with me to the grave. If they keep probing, it just might all come out." There are tears in her eyes as she continues. "If I lose my job, I might lose my kids. Please, please, stop them," she pleads.

"You've been doing fine," he says. "Just keep deflecting that line of questioning. Like you just did. Stay cool. Don't mention the nondisclosure agreement. That would only encourage them to dig deeper."

Upon their return, Tisch seems to have abandoned his interest in how she got the job, and moves on to other concerns. Finally Jansen's attorney signals he's finished.

Schubachs sighs with relief. She suppresses her deep desire to confront Jansen directly. Instead, she rises elegantly, determined to depart with the same reserve she brought into the room.

Now off the record, Tisch tosses a personal jab at the state's witness. "Whistle blowers are never popular in any profession."

Her brother, passive throughout the formal interrogation, quickly reacts. "Is that an attempt to intimidate the witness?"

Tisch backs off. The mounting tension in the room eases. "See you at the hearing. Thank you for your time."

"I'll be there," Dr. Schubachs assures him. She keeps her anxiety in check until she reaches her office. There she flops in her chair, begins breathing exercises to slow down her racing heart. She reflects out loud, "Carole, Carole, Carole, what have you gotten me into? Why did I ever take you on as a patient? You are not going to ruin my life or my career. I won't let you."

# 47

When Carole arrives for her next appointment, Dr. Schubachs's face is pale and drawn, her eyes filled with distant concerns. The patient wonders what might be going on in her therapist's life.

As the session moves on, Dr. Schubachs slowly recaptures her professional persona. The two spend time discussing Carole's new job and her father's deteriorating condition. Then the doctor moves on to her own agenda for the meeting.

"I've met Dr. Jansen now," the psychiatrist begins. "I'm still trying to figure out what you saw in him. I think we need to talk about your feelings toward Dr. Jansen."

Her patient stares at the floor. She falls into a prolonged silence as she struggles to articulate feelings that have changed over time. The clock ticks away precious wasted therapy time. In the stillness, Schubachs' mind drifts off to yesterday's deposition. She finds it difficult to focus on her patient's needs when her own are so great.

Carole finally breaks her silence. "In the beginning, I believed he really cared about my well-being. I thought he was trying to help me. When I told therapists about it, no one ever questioned me about it. I really never have had a chance to sort out my feelings."

"But you were raised with a very rigid moral code. Did you ever consider that sex with him might be morally wrong?"

"In my day no one really talk about sex. Not the nuns. Not my biology teacher. Not even my Mom. What I learned in parochial school was that it could land me in Hell. Sex was very scary for me. I didn't know how to get past that fear. I prayed about it a lot, but my fear didn't go away. I knew God made me a sexual creature. It's a part of being human I felt I had to deal with somehow. I knew I wasn't normal. People have sex. I had to come to terms with my fear. Crazy, huh?"

She goes on to explain that she'd heard of something called sex therapy. It's not like she was in love with the guy. She never even called him by his first name. She'd never touched him like lovers touch each other. He did the touching, the undressing. She thought she was doing the right thing.

"Believe me, sex with Dr. Jansen was harder for me to endure than any penance the convent imposed," Carole admits. Shame washes over her as flashbacks surge through her brain.

Then there's a shift in her demeanor.

"I've met the real Dr. Jansen. He doesn't care at all about my well-being—probably never did. He isn't even as tall as I remember him. When he lied about what he did, I actually felt sorry for him. What a coward he's turned out to be!"

The phone in the outer office interrupts the session. Schubachs apologizes. "I'm expecting an important call. I really need to take this. I'll be back."

While waiting, Carole pulls out a driver's license renewal form she recently received in the mail. It's different than others she's received. She has to answer questions about her mental state. Maybe because the police were involved with taking her to the hospital?

Two questions in particular pose a problem. Carole anticipates an honest answer might trigger trouble. It's not in her nature to lie so she circles yes to those two troublesome questions.

> Have you ever been hospitalized for a mental illness?
> Have you ever used a car for the purpose of committing suicide?

The patient debates on how to answer the second question. She did use the car when she drugged herself, but her dying in the car did not impose any danger to other people. When she regained consciousness, she drove home for less than a mile. There was no traffic on the road at the time, and it was a medical emergency.

She decides the best thing to do would be to ask Dr. Schubachs to enclose a letter to explain the whole situation, since the physician was required to sign the form.

Carole shudders. Losing her driving privileges would be a crippling blow. She couldn't visit her father in the hospital. She couldn't get the kids to places they need to go. She couldn't go grocery shopping. She couldn't get to her new job.

Dr. Schubachs returns in an agitated state from talking to her divorce lawyer. "I'm sorry but I am going to have to call this session short. I have an important legal matter that can't wait."

"No problem. I just need you to do something for me." Carole produces the DMV form and asks Dr. Schubachs to sign it. She explains her concern about answering yes to the suicide question and asks her therapist to please enclose a note explaining that she would never use her car to hurt other people. She mentions that the therapist is also required to sign the form, and since she herself has already signed and stamped it, could Dr. Schubachs please mail it.

"I'll be sure to take care of that," Dr. Schubachs assures her, as she absentmindedly slips the form into the patient's file.

Carole leaves confident the DMV matter is settled. After all she has a perfect driving record. She's never had any citation or even a parking ticket.

That's why she's shocked when a letter arrives a few weeks later informing her that her driver's license is being revoked.

She calls Dr. Schubachs to find out what happened. She reaches an answering machine as per usual so she leaves a message. Didn't the doctor send in the form as she promised to do?

As her panic swells, she turns to Jonathon for help. Her attorney promises to set up a hearing with the DMV to explain the situation. He assures her she can drive legally until after that takes place. "Calm down," he says, "you've got enough on your plate to deal with. I can take care of this."

"What a hellish day," Dr. Schubachs sighs as she collapses in that same office chair a week later.

Trouble began when she arrived at work and found the head of the department waiting in her office.

"Just a heads up," he began, in a conspiratorial tone. "There's a reporter nosing around. He got a leak from the DA's office about some alleged sexual misconduct here at the Mental Health Center." He paused to wipe his brow. "We're under close scrutiny here, Schubachs. That kind of publicity could kill us."

Then he glared at her in a way that suggested what was coming next was very personal. "Remember our nondisclosure agreement. I'd better not hear any mention of that. Not from you, or anyone else. That is, if you want to keep your job."

She blurted out loud, "Of course," while inside, her imagination spun wildly. What if that attorney brings it up in the hearing? He's been poking around in her employment history. What would she say then, if she's put under oath?

Next came the call from some unknown source. Raucous music pounded in her ears, a hissing snakelike sound was followed by a malicious voice screaming "whistleblower." Then came dead silence. It seemed like forever 'til the person hung up. That left her numb.

Then Jake's attorney called. The divorce wasn't going well. Jake wanted the house *and* the kids?

By the third strike, she was out. Not only have these events upended her equilibrium, they've also pushed back her scheduled appointments. So it's late by the time she picks up her messages, in no mood for nonsense from anyone. This has been a classic go-home-and-kick-the-dog kind of day. Good thing she's not a passive-aggressive person, or someone would pay.

So when she picks up Carole's irritated message, she overreacts. Damn. She did forget to mail that form to the DMV. It was a simple mistake, but Carole has a way of making her feel so incompetent. That suicide attempt of hers embarrassed Schubachs in front of her colleagues. She also felt like a failure when Carole cut herself right in the office. Now this.

While the psychiatrist can't do much about her boss, or an unidentified caller, or Jake, she's got power over Carole. She vows to exercise it. She develops a litany of grievances she harbors against Carole to justify her ballooning anger. "Damn you, Carole, people make mistakes. Even doctors do. We're human, too. That doesn't give you any right to talk to me in that tone of voice. I've had it with you."

At Carole's next session, Schubachs stomps into the office threatening, "You are on the verge of being terminated."

This totally unexpected threat triggers a violent reaction. Carole thinks to herself, shouldn't *she* be the angry one? She glares at her therapist, but doesn't dare voice the rage she feels.

Taken aback at the blazing fury she sees in Carole's eyes, Dr. Schubachs asks, "What are you thinking?"

Carole answers. Big mistake.

"I'm angry. Not so much because you didn't mail the form to the DMV. Jonathon is going to take care of that." She hesitates to continue. She's not good at telling people why she's angry, but talking is better than cutting herself, she reasons. "I'm absolutely furious you would threaten termination. With the hearing just weeks away? You would abandon me now?"

*Abandon.* Strikes a bell.

Dr. Schubachs realizes she just attacked Carole where she is most vulnerable. Three psychiatrists in a forensic consultation just days ago concurred that fear of abandonment is Carole's Achilles' heel.

The therapist knows she ought to apologize, assure Carole of her continuing support; but caught up in her own ambivalence, she doesn't. She's no longer sure she can continue to support Carole, not if it costs her her own family and her career.

Carole leaves Dr. Schubachs's office in a state of psychic shock. She tells herself this can't be happening. How could her therapist falter so close to the finish line?

Leanne and Jonathon. Abe and Jim. George and Oprah. The reporters who tell her story to the world. The women in the support group. They're her teammates but Schubachs is her coach. She lit the fire in Carole, told her the key to getting better was to address the sexual abuse head-on. She fueled her hope of recovery.

The two of them have traveled some pretty rough terrain together. Now, with the finish line in sight, how can her coach pull out, cut her feet out from under her? Who would be there to welcome her when she crosses the finish line? Who would share in her victory? When did Dr. Schubachs stop caring? And why? This—the sharpest betrayal yet.

Carole never felt so alone.

She holds her rage in check as she drives across town to her father's deathbed. For the third time this week, the family has been summoned to his bedside, only to have him bounce back. He won't last much longer. She needs to be with him. She must control her suicidal impulses. She cannot burden her family with more than they are already dealing with.

Once she arrives at the ICU, she calls Dr. Schubachs from a pay phone in the visitor's waiting room and apologizes. She begs her therapist to admit her to the Mental Health Center until her suicidal impulses subside. Her psychiatrist curtly refuses her request and hangs up on her.

Desperate for help, Carole then calls the private hospital where she was recently treated for her suicide attempt. She explains the current circumstances and asks to be temporarily admitted. They invite her to come in, and she does.

Safe inside the psychiatric unit, Carole's panic subsides. She can't hurt herself here. Eventually, with the help of a sedative, she collapses into a restless sleep, but awakens halfway through the night with a premonition that her father just passed away.

When her hospital appointed psychiatrist breaks the news of her father's passing the next morning, she's not surprised. What she is not prepared for is his other news. Dr. Schubachs just called to terminate Carole as her patient.

Overwhelmed by the serious nature of the news he must deliver an already suicidal patient, the man feels genuine compassion for Carole. She hears him comment to a nurse, "If she felt she had to terminate her, couldn't she have waited for a better time?" He searches for words to comfort his patient, but stumbles in the process. "With your grief over your father's death, you probably won't even miss her."

While she appreciates his awkward attempt to assuage her sorrow,

Carole feels both losses equally. How can she weigh one against the other? Both represent a permanent loss of important people in her life. Grief at her father's death may take center stage at the moment but it was expected. And her father did not choose to leave; he wrestled with death until it finally overcame his weakened body. The loss of her therapist was deliberate, unexpected, and far more hurtful.

Dad was never a quitter; neither is she. She vows her testimony at the hearing will serve as a witness to what her father taught her about life and service.

Of all the kids, she had been closest to him, but confined to a psych hospital, she cannot be with her siblings as they choose her father's coffin and plan his funeral. They recognize that special bond by asking her to deliver a poem at his service. The funeral falls appropriately on the feast of Francis of Assisi, his patron saint. Was Francis not the saint who prayed:

> *Grant that I may*
> *not so much seek to be consoled as to console*
> *To be understood as to understand*
> *To be loved as to love*
> *For it is in giving that we receive*
> *It is in pardoning that we are pardoned*
> *And it is in dying that we are born to eternal life*

Could this be Dad's message from the grave?

Following the funeral, Abe Friedman and Jim Anderson show up at the hospital with a card of condolence. It is touching. They inquire if Carole will still be able to go through with the hearing now that Dr. Schubachs has terminated her?

The sting of her therapist's betrayal is still fresh. Now it is public and sharp.

She overcomes the shame that threatens to cripple her. "There's something bigger at stake here than Dr. Schubachs," she says. "Speaking truth to power carries a heavy price. She should have known that. I assure you—I'll be there."

# 48

The day of the hearing, Carole chooses her wardrobe thoughtfully, knowing she will be judged as much by how she presents herself as by anything she says. She selects a long-sleeved white blouse, a navy-blue business suit, dress shoes with slightly raised heels, even applies a bit of lipstick. When she evaluates her appearance in the floor-length mirror, she decides she looks professional and mentally competent.

Breakfast odors are nauseating today, the children's chatter irritating. Still, she manages a smile for Arvid as he leaves for class. He offers her a thumbs up.

Leanne and Jonathon wait in the foyer of the state building, relaxed, confident, and welcoming.

"Hey, there, am I glad to see you," Carole says, trying to swallow the lump in her throat. "I need to see some friendly faces."

"How's it going so far?" Jonathon inquires.

"Don't know," she says. "I chose not to be here except when I'm needed as a witness. I can't handle too much negativity right now," she adds, somewhat apologetically.

"That's understandable," Leanne says. "Let's get a cup of coffee," she suggests. "Abe's waiting for us in the cafeteria."

It's easy to spot Friedman in the sparsely occupied room. Today, the state's attorney is strictly businesslike, and he gets right to the point. "Just to bring you up to date. Dr. Schubachs and Sister Amelia both testified yesterday but they're not done. We should finish Sister Amelia's testimony this morning. Schubachs will be back tomorrow. She's balking a bit. She complains she's got other patients to see. But at least she's holding up her end as a witness."

"I'm glad for that," Carole mumbles.

"She's been subpoenaed, so she'll be back whether she wants to or not," Friedman assures her.

"When you finish here, the three of you can wait in the hall. I'll get you when it's time, probably mid-morning." Friedman then leaves for the hearing that's about to convene.

A half hour later, the three of them make their way to a hallway bench outside the room where the hearing is in session. Alone with her thoughts, Carole time-travels back to that October day thirty-some years ago when she aspired to be a Wonder Woman. A magic bracelet and a golden tiara would be great right now. She doesn't feel particularly Amazonian at the moment.

Finally, the door opens. Friedman invites them in. He tells them the examiner ordered a 15-minute recess. They need to be in place when he returns.

Carole finds the room far less imposing than the county courtroom where Jonathon argued the civil suit. There's no mosaic of a blind-folded Justice, no judicial bench or jury box, no observers or reporters. There's only an American flag next to the state flag, both symbols of a duly regulated society.

This is just an ordinary meeting room. Two conference tables face one in the middle, reserved for the hearing examiner. A court reporter is positioned to his right; a witness chair is placed to his left.

Defense attorney Ben Tisch converses quietly with Jansen, who slouches in his chair, his long legs extending far beyond the edge of the table in a typical posture that conveys arrogance, self-righteousness and indifference. Carole wonders why she ever trusted this guy.

Attorney Friedman and investigator Anderson prep Carole briefly, then concentrate on their notes. Leanne hugs Carole, Jonathon does a thumbs up, and the two select a strategic spot where they can observe what is going on and Carole can see them from the witness chair.

When the side door opens, everyone rises. The hearing examiner checks if everyone is ready, paying closest attention to the court reporter. She nods assent, and the hearing resumes.

Friedman begins. "I'd like to call Carole Thornton to the witness stand."

Absent a formal bailiff, the court reporter officiates with the traditional legal ritual. "Do you solemnly swear to tell the truth, the whole truth, and nothing but the truth, so help you God?"

"I do."

Carole takes her place in the witness chair.

Finally. Her day in court—well, sort of. First and foremost she's a state witness. While every part of her wants to tell the story in her own way, today attorney Friedman decides which parts are relevant to the state's case against Jansen. Someday, she vows, she'll tell it her own way, but not today.

Friedman, commissioned as he is to protect citizens from gross medical malpractice, has coached his star witness well to achieve that end. He's explained his agenda. For three long—probably arduous—days, he will present facets of the case that support Carole's claim that sexual misconduct took place in therapy. Next, he will show that Jansen's misconduct resulted in substantial psychological damage to his patient. Finally, he will argue that Jansen's license should be revoked because his behavior poses a serious threat to those who might seek his professional services.

As an experienced prosecutor, Friedman anticipates that the defendant will portray Carole in as negative a light as possible. He warned her in advance, "Be prepared to have your sanity and your motives called into question." His job, he explained, was to steer her through a strange juxtaposition in American jurisprudence: the assumption of innocence is awarded to the accused, while it is often the victim witness who is put on trial.

He cautioned Carole that attorney Ben Tisch might claim she was psychotic at the time and just imagined the sexual activity. Should that argument fall flat, he'll probably claim she hates all therapists, and acts out of revenge. Or he might claim that the witness is plain lying. Carole is prepared for all three scenarios.

"Please state your full name and spell it slowly for the clerk to enter it into the records," the examiner orders as soon as everyone is settled in.

Formalities aside, Friedman begins his interrogation in earnest. "Why did you initially seek therapy with Dr. Jansen?"

Carole fills in her background story. Sister Amelia referred her to Dr. Jensen at the time of a roommate's suicide attempt because the therapist feared copycat behavior on her part. Even though she was not suicidal at the time, the nun sent her to a psychiatrist who could prescribe medication, something a psychologist could not do. Amelia felt Carole needed to relate to a male therapist because she had known very few men during her high school and college years spent in convent living.

Friedman next directs attention to Carole's relationship with Jansen. In response to his direction, she relates how early on she made progress in adjusting to life outside of the convent. When she came to trust her therapist, he seduced her into sexual intimacies as a "cure" for her fear of sex.

How could she have trusted that man sitting across the room only half paying attention?

"Why did you leave therapy?" Friedman prompts

She describes how she met her husband-to-be and found strength in that relationship to finally break Jansen's hold on her.

"Did you have any further contact with Dr. Jansen?" Friedman inquires.

She reports the brief telephone encounter around the time of her wedding. The officiating priest insisted she produce a letter from her psychiatrist to verify her she was psychologically fit for marriage. She called Jansen to ask for a letter.

"How did he respond?"

"At first, he advised me to 'screw the Church'—his words, not mine. 'Get married somewhere else. Go to a Justice of the Peace.' He hated the Catholic Church and repeatedly tried to undermine my faith. I told him it was important to me to be married in the Church. Reluctantly, he agreed to write the letter. That's the only contact we've had until I filed this complaint with the licensing board. Since then I've seen him at several depositions, but never spoke to him directly."

As she testifies, she observes Jansen's demeanor. To her, he looks so pathetic. The guy knows the truth. Why can't he just admit what he did? Why is he making her prove it? What a jerk!

After Friedman questions his star witness, he turns her over to the defense attorney, knowing full well his opponent will attempt to discredit her.

The defendant's "expert" psychiatrist-for-pay Shaun Kelly is an icon in the local courts, noted for his arrogance, dogmatic pronouncements, and signature cowboy boots. He'd asked to interview Carole before advising Tisch on how to proceed. The hearing examiner disallowed his request, stating it wouldn't be necessary given the multitude of mental health professionals who have already interviewed her.

So Kelly read Carole's case records over the weekend. That limited information suggested a strategy for the defense to use in its cross-examination. So the man's presence is felt in the room, even if he's not physically present. He suggests Tisch keep Carole talking as much as possible, applying enough pressure to make her reveal her mental instability.

Tisch begins his cross-examination by challenging Carole's mental state at the time of the alleged abuse. "Could you explain why you were on Sparine back then?"

Friedman requests a moment to consult with his witness before she answers. He muffles the microphone as he speaks. In a voice dripping with sarcasm, he says, "Their so-called 'expert' testified yesterday that you were psychotic at the time the alleged abuse occurred. He claimed Sparine is used to treat psychosis."

Now that Carole understands the implication of the question, she knows exactly how to answer Tisch.

"Yes, I was taking Sparine when I first saw Jansen. After my roommate's suicide attempt, a psychiatrist I never met prescribed it at Sister Amelia's request. She wanted it as a stopgap measure to ward off any copycat behavior on my part, even though I was not suicidal at the time."

"But you were on it, right?" Tisch interrupts.

"Yes. Briefly. But during my first session with Dr. Jansen, he said I didn't need such strong medication. He took me off it and prescribed a milder anti-anxiety drug and an anti-depressant instead."

Tisch next attempts to establish that Carole hates therapists. "Isn't it true you put pins in a doll, then told a fellow patient that's what you'd like to do to Dr. Mielke?"

Carole chuckles, nervously. "Yes, I did."

"And why did you do that?"

"If you're suggesting I practice some kind of voodoo, I don't. I was simply expressing irritation at Dr. Mielke's Freudian approach in therapy. So often, I felt him dismiss me as an hysterical female. My roommate fully understood my frustration."

The prolonged grilling goes on for an hour until the hearing examiner finally calls a break.

In the hall, Friedman voices frustration over Tisch's line of questioning. "Kelly's behind this. Now I know why he wears those iconic cowboy boots to court," he mutters. "He needs them to wade through all the shit he spews."

When the session resumes, Friedman moves to the second point he must prove: namely, that Jansen's sexual misconduct caused Carole serious injury. He delves as gently and professionally as he can into Carole's past, raising painfully intimate questions. He reviews her subsequent hospitalizations, self-inflicted injuries, suicide attempts, and numerous therapies. He even brings up her prolonged participation in community mental health support groups.

To counteract any possible suggestion that Jansen's technique was a legitimate, successful treatment for sexual dysfunction, he asks about her current sex life. "Are you able to have an orgasm?" he asks.

Carole freezes. She never expected to address *this*. Not in front of *him*. She blushes at this invasion of her privacy. "Yes, I can. What I experience is not frigidity, it's sexual aversion."

The state's attorney has covered all the key items on his agenda. One thing is left. After all she has been through, Friedman feels he owes Carole her own voice. He poses one simple question. "Ms. Thornton, is there anything you want to say to Dr. Jansen?"

Carole looks directly at her former therapist and addresses him as one human being to another. Angry that she has been portrayed as a psychotic liar, she says exactly what's uppermost on her mind.

"I dare you to look me in the eye and say this never happened."

The court reporter's *click-click-click* comes to a halt.

Unwilling to meet Carole's piercing gaze, Dr. Jansen slouches even lower. A metamorphosis takes place. He becomes the killer caught with the smoking gun in his hand, the little boy caught with his hand in the cookie jar. In the deafening silence, his body language screams "GUILTY".

Tisch recovers from a momentary stupor, leans over, and advises his client not to respond.

*Too late, Ben. He already has*, she thinks to herself.

As she leaves the stand, Friedman congratulates Carole on a job well done. He explains it will be weeks, maybe months before the hearing examiner delivers his recommendation to the Board. He promises to call her as soon as the results come in.

# 49

The lake wears many faces. Today it is dark, gloomy, foreboding. Waves crash relentlessly against the breakwater as a storm brews in the distance. A lone figure moves cautiously along the dock until he locates the yacht he's seeking in the prevailing fog. Tisch descends into the boat as he has many times before.

Jansen looks up from polishing the railings of the *Lucy*. "Welcome aboard, mate," he shouts.

"Strange place to hold a meeting," Tisch replies. "Isn't it a bit early in the season to be out on the lake?" he asks.

"It's safe to talk here," Jansen explains. "No one can eavesdrop.

Besides I thought I'd spend time here while I still have the *Lucy*. I stand to lose her, don't I?" Jansen's shoulders slump in defeat. "My ex isn't taking this well. She argues, if I fuck my patients, what's to stop me from doing the same thing to my daughter. Ben, you know I'd never hurt Lucy!"

"I take it Janine's not buying your innocence then?"

"Naw. She always knows when I'm lying."

"So what keeps you from just telling the truth?"

"Lucy. I'm her hero."

"You won't be much longer, I'm afraid."

"Get off my case," Jansen spews.

Tempted to respond, *I'd love to*, Tisch holds his professional tongue. "So what's your game plan, Harry? How do you plan to stay afloat?"

"That's why I set up this meeting. Tell me what to do next."

"You're never going to convince anyone Carole's making this up. Even your own wife believes her." Tisch pulls at his beard as he searches for some legal loophole. In the lake's wild turmoil, he spots a sea gull on the prowl. The bird of prey dives and resurfaces with a silver fish in its mouth.

"If you lose this case, and it looks like that's a strong possibility, you might have a chance with the court of appeals. Decisions at the appeals level are based on legal technicalities."

The attorney summarizes the legal implications of the initial hearing, which focused on proving that sexual misconduct occurred and that it caused serious damage to the patient. "If the hearing examiner believes that the sexual misconduct occurred and that it damaged Carole, he will probably recommend that the state revoke your license," he warns.

The court of appeals will focus on whether due process was followed in the proceedings. But this is an administrative issue, not something adjudicated in a civil court or a criminal court. So it's unclear if the statute of limitations precludes disciplinary action for misconduct that occurred some eighteen years ago, Tisch explains.

"I'm willing to argue the statute question," Tisch offers reluctantly.

"It's something I can live with." In spite of his great distaste for serving as caretaker for this badly impaired physician, Tisch books himself to manage the appeal should they need it. He substitutes Jansen's hold on him for a more heartfelt mission to provide for his godchild's economic well-being.

A giant wave rocks the boat, knocking Jansen's drink out of his hand. He lets it lie on the deck unattended. Something more important is on his mind.

"So what do I do 'til the decision comes in?" the psychiatrist inquires.

"Keep practicing. Your license remains valid during the appeal process. People have short memories, Harry. Some folks don't ever read the paper. Your name won't mean a thing to them." Another popular solution pops into his head. "Censured physicians often just move to another state to practice. Hmm . . . you've got some property up north. Maybe you should open shop up there. I'm sorry, Harry, I really am." He feels compassion for his one-time friend, mixed with remorse for his own courtroom failure and relief that the initial hearing is over. "You can rebuild your life, Harry. Other people do." He catches himself about to utter, *Find a good therapist.* That advice probably wouldn't sit well right now.

# *50*

Carole is folding the family laundry at the kitchen table when the wall phone rings She crosses the room to answer.

"Hi, Carole; Abe. Is this a good time to talk?"

Her eyes open wide in anticipation. It's the call she's been expecting for months. Finally. "I'll make time. What's up?"

"It's been awhile. I'll bet you think we forgot about you?"

Carole rolls her eyes. "Not really, Abe. One thing I've learned: the legal process takes time. It's already consumed more than two years of my life. I'm anxious to hear how the case will be resolved. I hope that's why you're calling."

"You're going to like the news."

Carole feels a quickening of her pulse. Quite subconsciously she crosses her fingers.

"The hearing examiner presented his recommendation to the board yesterday."

"And..."

"The board voted unanimously to accept it."

"Come on, Abe, don't keep me in suspense. What did he decide?"

"Hmm . . . let me see," Abe teases. He selects an appropriate authoritative voice to read. "I recommend that the board revoke Dr. Jansen's license to practice medicine in this state."

Then he says in a more conversational tone, "The findings are complex. I think you'll want to read them yourself."

"Give me a summary," she pleads.

"The court believes the abuse occurred. The examiner refutes the testimony of Jansen's 'expert' witnesses. Sparine was used for conditions other than psychosis in the '60's."

"So I'm not crazy...I wasn't just imagining it." Carole laughs to relieve her tension.

Her joy is somewhat subdued. She can't help feeling compassion for Jansen, who will pay a heavy price. If only he had been honest, shown a bit of remorse...

"Are you still there?"

"Yes, I'm just taking it all in. So, it's finally over?"

"Don't count on that. Expect an appeal. You won't be involved in that, though. Everything from this point forward involves legal technicalities. Whatever happens, no one will ever again dispute whether or not this really happened."

"You can't imagine what that means to me," Carole says as she wipes away the tears streaming down her cheeks.

"I can tell you what finally convinced the examiner," Abe adds. "He refers to the moment I asked if there was anything you wanted to say to Jansen..."

"Yeah, you caught me off guard. We hadn't prepared for that."

"I'm glad we didn't plan ahead. You spoke from your heart. It was so genuine. The hearing examiner put great weight on Jansen's body language. He looked so guilty.

"Guess I'll never forget that," Carole says.

"I'll send you a copy of the written report before your name is redacted from the public record. Feel free to share it with anyone you want, but we will keep our promise to never release your name."

"Thanks, Abe."

Abe and Carole both sense a parting of the ways.

"If there is anything else I can do, please call. And thanks, Carole, for what you've done."

"Thank you, Abe. Please thank Jim, too, for a super job in digging up the facts of the case."

Carole whispers her thanks to God as she returns to folding the clean laundry. She can't wait to share the news. A momentary pang taints the victory. This should be the time to share her victory with Dr. Schubachs, but that will never happen.

When the legal document arrives by special delivery, Carole is selective about what she reads. She skips testimony from therapists. Labels hurt; she wants nothing more to do with them. She puts the Examiner's findings in the lockbox of her heart and in a personal file. Someday she will read it in its entirety—someday, when she takes time to tell the story in her own way.

# 51

As Dr. Marjorie Bemmer enters her clinic, she scarcely acknowledges the receptionist's warm greeting and the proffered cup of steaming coffee. Her focus is on some unfinished business she has postponed too long. She closes the door and dials Dr. Betty Schubachs' number.

She moves directly to the purpose of her call. "How'd the Hearing go?"

"I really don't care to discuss it," Schubachs snaps. "It's over, done with."

"Do you think it's over and done with for Carole?"

Schubachs' lips tighten around a clenched jaw. She dismisses the older woman's comment with a callous "Frankly, I don't care. I discharged her. She's not my problem anymore."

The image of Pontius Pilate washing his hands flits through Bemmer's mind. "That's a bit cold. In our clinic, we care. We go to court with our clients and we support them afterwards."

Bent on turning the younger psychiatrist's failure into a learning experience, Bemmer refuses to drop the matter. "When you advised Carole, didn't you consider the tough, real life challenges she would have to face? I'm sure she assumed you would have her back in the process," she says. "I doubt she'll ever trust a therapist again, so I won't be her therapist, but I will help coordinate the professional conference she's planning," she adds.

Sensing that any chance of ever partnering with Bemmer is vanishing faster than maple leaves in a November gale, Schubachs adopts an offensive posture. "I'm no longer interested in a partnership with Women and Families. I'll leave the politicking to you."

She wants to slam the phone down but caution freezes her hand in place. Alienating Bemmer would not be a wise career move. Still, she's had enough of the older woman's chiding. She excuses herself. "I don't have time for this. I need to go. I have a patient waiting."

"I think you need to make time, Betty. For your own sake . . . and the sake of your future patients. "

"Good bye."

Dr. Schubachs cradles the phone, then puts her head down on the desk and sobs. Whoever said, "Time heals all wounds?" Not true; it never does.

Eventually, she staggers to her private bathroom, where she sees a very distraught image in the mirror. She washes her tears away, applies a trace of lipstick, and adjusts her disheveled hair. "Physician, heal thyself," she mutters. Then she adds, "I have yet to figure out how to do that."

She turns to her patients to regain emotional equilibrium. Today, she welcomes the boredom of daily routine.

# 52

Six months pass before Carole gets a final call from Abe Friedman. "The court of appeals ruled in Jansen's favor. The judge decided the statute of limitations applies to administrative cases as well as civil and criminal ones."

Carole holds her breath. She doesn't know what to say, and Abe doesn't know how to interpret her silence.

"Sorry, Carole," he says in a genuine attempt to console her. "I really am."

Though deeply disappointed, Carole reminds Abe, "Jansen's behavior was tried in the court of public opinion. Eventually change will come. People will demand it."

"This isn't over yet, Carole. The state medical board voted unanimously to appeal his ruling to the state supreme court. Imposing a statute of limitations on disciplinary action would truly hinder our mission. It's our job to protect the public. We're not giving up yet."

"Thanks, Abe. I appreciate that." She sighs. She's learned to take difficult things in stride. "I have no control over what happens in the court. But I do have control over some things. I can educate the public and I can support survivors. That's where I'll direct my energy now."

Months pass. Carole is now fully employed. Arvid, with his training completed, finds work in his new field. On one pleasant spring evening, Carole and Arvid sit in their living room perusing the paper while the kids play outside. Arvid is caught up with news of Opening Day, while Carole focuses on local news.

"It's the zeitgeist," she exclaims out loud.

Arvid looks up. "What? Zeitgeist? Haven't heard that word used since history class. Wasn't it the 'spirit of our times'?"

"Yes, yes," Carole replies. "People are finally paying more attention to sexual abuse by those in positions of power. But you know what, Arvid? One important voice is strangely silent in this. I can't ignore that any more."

Arvid tosses the sports page aside, better to focus on what's bugging his wife.

"And who might that be?"

"The Church. *My* Church. Sister Amelia surrendered her license for one year. One year! That year is just about up. Now what happens? Will her religious order just let her continue counseling young women? What oversight is there?"

The gentle spring breeze has morphed into a strong wind. Conscious of the storm brewing in the distance, Arvid gets up to shut the windows.

He settles back down with a sigh. "This will never end for you, will it, Carole?"

"It's not ending. Look. This article in today's paper caught my attention. Teachers at a parochial school just a few miles from here were fired for reporting a priest abuser to authorities."

"Hmmm…" Arvid mulls that over. "Fired? Didn't the teachers do what they're supposed to do?"

As a convert, he struggles with the ins and outs of the Catholic Church. But teacher terminations—that he can relate to. In a parochial school there wouldn't be a union to fight for teachers' rights. That alone bothers him.

"I don't get it," Carole continues. "My Church should be leading the crusade to stop sexual abuse of vulnerable people. It's not. I need to find a way to grab the archbishop's attention."

Looking out the window, Arvid sees the kids heading for home as raindrops begin to fall. No need to call them in.

"Haven't you done enough already, Carole?" he asks. "It's been almost five years since you started this crusade."

"It's never *enough* as long as the abuse goes on. Obviously the Church is not on board."

"Come on, Carole. Enough." He sighs. "Can't we just lead a normal life, enjoy our kids? Besides this case is probably just a fluke, a maverick."

"Don't kid yourself. There's plenty of opportunity for abuse in a Church setting. Who even talks about it? Hmmm ... maybe I should ask the archbishop to endorse my conference."

"Ah, a reasonable solution. That's something doable. Go for it."

Carole's voice rises a pitch or two. She's now super alert, breathing fast, as she morphs into a Wonder Woman committed to taking on an Amazonian task that lies before her.

"Priests and nuns represent the Divine! Society gives them a sacred status. Think of the power they wield. Sexual abuse by a nun or a priest is incredibly damaging. I should know."

"No argument here, Carole. But churches hate scandals. It diminishes their credibility. You watch. That priest will be transferred to another diocese, maybe another state, where nobody knows anything about his past. That's all that'll happen."

"You're right, Arvid. Church leaders protect their image religiously, pardon the pun." Carole shakes the newspaper furiously. "But this. Teachers getting fired when they ought to be applauded for doing their job? This has got to stop."

As she lies in bed that night Carole replays her conversation with Arvid. She recalls Mother Superior's response to her own complaint about Sister Amelia. There was no letter of apology, no compassion, no accountability. Worst of all, there was no recognition that the order itself had created the environment in which such abuse could occur. Their cover-up is what drove her teens away from the Church. Hypocrisy just doesn't fly with youth.

Days later, a notice in the paper catches her attention. The archbishop is going to hold a community get-together to discuss the new liturgical celebration he plans to implement. The question and answer session will take place at the cathedral the following Saturday. The public is encouraged to bring forth their concerns.

"I got it," she shares with Arvid. "I'll attend that presentation. Maybe I can talk to him afterwards. I hear he likes feedback from his audience."

"Sure you're up to tackling an institution as big as the Church?"

"After what we've been through, do you doubt me? I'll give it a try."

"I'm sure you will," he sighs.

The cathedral with its red brick façade, stained-glass windows and century-old bell tower is located on the fringes of downtown, attracting a mix of both traditional and progressive parishioners. As Carole takes her seat, the familiar smells of beeswax candles and incense remind her of her past when she tended to the altar and sacristy after school. There's a buzz in the wooden pews as people gather, but everyone quiets down when the bell chimes out the hour and the archbishop takes the podium.

Because of her greater concern for social justice than liturgical ceremony, Carole only half-listens to the presentation. She focuses more on the archbishop than on what he has to say. The prelate is stately, speaks eloquently, and vacillates between a political and pastoral persona. Understandable. He must appease both the liberal and conservative factions in his audience or risk losing parishioners. Her hands are clammy, her stomach churns, and her heart races. She feels like David preparing to face a giant Goliath, but she plans to keep cool and proceed cautiously.

When the presentation ends, a line forms of those who wish to address the archbishop personally. She heads to the back of the line, seeking privacy for what she plans to share. When it's finally her time to speak, Carole blurts out, "When are you going to do something about priests who abuse children?" Her tone is more accusatory than she intends.

A shocked expression sweeps over the prelate's face, replaced by irritation. His warm pastoral demeanor shifts to a more political one. He straightens to his tallest stature, Goliath ready to defend himself against an upstart peasant shepherd. He looks down his nose, and responds in his most patronizing voice. "These are such, um, delicate matters..." he suggests.

She draws in a sharp breath. *Bullshit! Who knows more about these "delicate matters" than she does?* But knowing that men don't like angry women, she makes a Herculean effort to contain her rage. She loses the battle. Blood rushes to her face, and her eyes become wide and glaring as her anger escalates.

Intimidated by this livid middle-aged woman, the prelate shifts his approach. "Give me times and dates and I'll do something," he assures her.

He then spins around to seek refuge beyond the sacristy door that separates the worship space from a rather mundane dressing room. Safely away and paralyzed with fear, he takes a hanky from his pocket to wipe away the sweat running down his face.

He prays for guidance. It comes in the form of a memory—a conversation he'd overheard between two cardinals. Their tête-à-tête in the men's room went something like this.

"I'll grant you celibacy is an ongoing challenge," the younger one said. "It has been since it was first imposed in 1139. Some priests choose affairs on the side, but going after kids? Doesn't that bother you? Lonely people who don't get much attention from home are such easy targets. They like being special to a priest or nun."

"They lap up the attention, and then call foul?" the older man responded. "Aren't they equally responsible for what happens?"

"Hmmm," the first one replied. "Can't quite agree with that. Who's supposed to be in charge of the relationship? But put that question aside for the moment, when abuse surfaces in a parish, what are we to do?"

"Transfer time." The older prelate wiped his hands together in a gesture of dismissal, as one might do in brushing away unwanted crumbs on one's fingers. He glanced around the room and lowered his voice to almost a whisper before continuing. "In the worst case-scenario—golf with the lawyers most loyal to the faith, if you know what I mean." He chuckles, then continues, "If we don't put the kibosh on these ridiculous complaints, why, anyone with an axe to grind could make wild and costly claims against Mother Church. Soon they'd be dragging the nuns to court, too. How ludicrous would that be?"

When the older man heard agitation in the younger man's voice, the cardinal defended his position. "We're responsible for maintaining moral order. That's what the world expects of us. If we lose our credibility, who's to lead the flock? Aquinas said it best. Sometimes we must choose the lesser of two evils."

Great advice, the archbishop decides. Now he knows just how to handle "the problem."

But peace eludes him. What if those damn reporters keep digging? If they find out about his Michael, how will that pan out?

His Roman collar grows limp as sweat flows profusely down his neck. He yanks it off, stuffs it in his pocket and leaves the sacristy. Back at the chancery, he heads directly to his office, shuts the door and puts a "DO NOT DISTURB" sign in place. Then he picks up the phone and dials Michael's number.

No Michael picking up. Michael must be working in the college library as part of his work-study program at the moment, the prelate concludes. He leaves a message. "Michael, it's me. We gotta talk. Call me."

How much hush money could he offer Michael to keep their relationship from the press? He checks his account.

# 53

Though visibly shaken by her encounter with the archbishop, Carole leaves convinced they have at least cracked the door. She'll send him times and dates as he requested, and see how he responds when she describes her experience with Sister Amelia. Once he knows, will he take the necessary steps to stop any further abuse?

An internal voice warns, *Be cautious. Start slow.* Maybe ask him to endorse the upcoming conference?

Acting with due diligence before contacting him, Carole does her research. The psychology board's leniency in dealing with Sister Amelia never really made any sense to her. She calls Abe Friedman for an explanation. It turns out the nun's lawyer found a legal loophole. He argued that it wasn't unequivocally a professional relationship, since money was never exchanged. On the other hand, the state's attorney countered that money is rarely involved in church-related counseling. Furthermore, the nun had testified she was acting in her role as therapist. The two sides negotiated for a one-year's suspension, which Abe felt was barely a slap on the wrist.

Carole forgets to breathe as she listens to Abe. Without a fresh intake of oxygen, she literally begins to choke on the news. "Just when I thought the nun was being forthright."

After hanging up, she weighs the special consideration given to the nun. Scheduled appointments with a nun psychologist in a therapy office on a college campus—not a therapy relationship? Money isn't what establishes a relationship. Time, place, position, and agenda do.

Now for sure she is concerned. Without proper oversight, the nun might indeed go on to abuse other young women on the college campus. She has to stop her.

In a carefully thought-out letter Carole requests the archbishop's intervention. She tells him about her effort to educate people, including professionals, at an upcoming conference, the first one in the nation designed to raise awareness of sexual abuse in counseling relationships. She explains that the YWCA will host the event, and the names of co-sponsoring agencies will appear on the brochure. So far there are 15—predominately mental health associations and women's organizations—offering their support.

She includes the conference agenda and background on the professional presenters, which includes social worker Elaine Christof from the Detroit Drop-In Clinic, nationally recognized for its leadership in exposing the problem. Carole stars one item: a panel of survivors will share their stories, providing attendees with a rare opportunity to learn how abuse impacts people's lives.

"No one can wipe out the tragedies of the past," she concludes in her letter. "We can only work to prevent such tragedy in the future." She anxiously awaits the archbishop's response, and holds off printing the brochure in hopes he will also endorse it. Isn't this in keeping with the mission of the Church to provide moral leadership?

Carole and a coworker are sitting in their respective desks going over paperwork when Kathryn gets up, crosses the room, and hands Carole an envelope.

"This is for you," Kathryn says. "Came in today's mail. Look at the return address. The Archdiocesan Office. Wow. What's that all about?"

"Finally. I've been waiting for that." She whispers a quick prayer, reaches into her desk for a letter opener, and slits open the envelope. "I'm way to nervous to read this, Kathryn. Do me a big favor? Read it and tell me what it says?"

Kathryn's face turns from serious to solemn as she peruses the correspondence. When she hesitates to share the contents of the letter, Carole knows the news is not good. She prepares herself for the worst.

"So sorry, Carole. The prelate won't endorse the conference. I know how important that is to you. He claims he relies on Catholic social workers to keep him informed on mental health issues." She grimaces. "Guess he doesn't need us."

Crushed, Carole slumps in her chair, and gives herself time to absorb the rejection. She begins to process her disappointment. "Sounds to me that he doesn't want interference from 'outsiders'."

"Sounds like it," Kathryn agrees. "What a tight-knit, closed-minded institution. Don't the rest of us know anything?"

"But, Kathryn, I'm not an outsider. I spent ten years in a convent, I taught five years in a parochial school, my sister is a nun." She thinks to herself, *Not to mention as a kid I cleaned the sacristy and sanctuary every single day. I got up early to sing at the 7 A.M. Mass before school. My parents headed many church committees. My Dad served as an usher and commentator. My Mom nursed the sick nuns, Dad tended to their household problems, and I ran errands for them. I'm not an outsider.*

"Damn," her coworker says. "You don't deserve this, Carole. You're trying to right a serious wrong. BUT you're a woman in a patriarchal church where female voices are traditionally silenced. You must feel so betrayed."

"Women teach, run hospitals, care for orphans, the aged and the poor!" Carole says. "When you think about it, women's service to the Church is double that of men's. We don't deserve this kind of treatment. Why do I keep hoping things will change? It's just hard to let go of a dream."

Kathryn hesitates to share the archbishop's closing words, which she knows will only add to the pain the prelate has already inflicted. She tries to soften the blow. "This is gonna hurt, Carole, but I think you need to hear the rest. He ended the letter with this. 'I do hope that the hurts of the past can also be buried. Otherwise, it can look as if one is also seeking a bit of vengeance.

"+May God bless you.+'"

Carole is absolutely stunned. If sexual misconduct by therapists and counselors rapes the human psyche, a church cover-up rapes the very soul of humankind. She cannot allow this to go on. The church of her youth was a haven where troubled souls found compassion, inspiration, moral clarity, and encouragement. She likens this archbishop's hurtful response to the spear thrust into the heart of Jesus after he was already dead.

"If he thinks he is protecting the Archdiocese, he's not, not really," Carole says. "If the Church chooses to blame victims while it shelters perpetrators, it's on course for self-destruction."

"I agree," Kathryn says. "Then convents and monasteries, schools and church pews will become empty relics of the past. Shit. Such hypocrisy!"

"I must warn him," she counters. "He must not let this happen. Not to my Church."

She takes the letter from her coworker, stares long and hard at the letterhead. She wipes away her angry tears, then rereads it to make sure they haven't misinterpreted his words. They haven't.

"Bury the hurt? Secrets like this destroy lives. You know what Maya Angelou wrote? 'There is no greater agony then bearing an untold story inside you.'" Carole walks to the window and looks out across the lake, then continues her rant. "Tell me, Kathryn. How could he possibly view an educational endeavor as 'seeking a bit of vengeance'?"

Then she vows, holding up the mocked-up brochure. "This will go on without the Archbishop's support. It may lack his endorsement, but the conference has great support from the community at large. I know it will be a success."

And it is. Over two hundred people attend.

Once the conference is over, Carole turns her attention back to winning the support of her church. She brainstorms on best ways to capture the archbishop's attention.

As a toddler, Mom taught her that when she hurt someone, she needed to say 'sorry' and make up for what she did. She had to promise not to repeat the offense. Mom said things weren't all better until she did. The nuns reinforced that lesson year after year in catechism classes and in playground disagreements at her parochial school. It was a simple but powerful path to justice. How can she get the arch-bishop to understand that?

She comes up with a strategy.

In his leadership role, the archbishop doesn't just bear moral responsibility for the archdiocese, he also carries fiscal responsibility. Money talks. Perhaps if she presents the harm to victims in monetary terms, he'll get it. Maybe he'll listen.

In her follow-up correspondence, she describes the financial cost to her family and asks the archbishop to pay her outstanding therapy bill amounting to $25,000. "It's a justice issue," she reminds him, "to right a terrible wrong."

This time he writes, "I am puzzled why you feel that the Archdio-cese should somehow make reparation for something a nun may have done. It simply does not seem very logical to me, but strangely emotional."

Carole is not too surprised at his response. The money angle was meant to get his attention and to suggest maybe he ought to consider the financial implications for ignoring the issue of sexual abuse. Per-haps it had struck a nerve. Though she anticipated he would reject her request, she did not anticipate the judgment that accompanies it.

"It is difficult to see how one can toss all the blame to one party and assume none oneself. My hope and prayer is that you would be freed from this obsession and come to know a loving, forgiving, and caring God."

Carole rejects the typical blame-the-victim language women have heard since the beginning of time. She shields herself against the cleric's attempt to project guilt onto her. Obviously the archbishop does not understand the abuse of power and doesn't want to. Maybe someday he'll get it, but he's not receptive now.

Still not willing to give up on a church that means so much to her, Carole takes the matter one step higher on the ecclesiastical ladder.

She writes to the papal nuncio, formal representative of the Vatican, who resides in Washington, D.C.

He passes the buck downwards.

"While I appreciate very much your interest in bringing this matter to my attention, I would encourage you to continue in your effort to resolve this matter in conjunction with the Archbishop, who has been entrusted by the Holy Father with the responsibility for the pastoral care of the Archdiocese."

Though devastated by the ecclesiastical blockade she faces, Carole refuses to admit defeat. She addresses the Church's hypocrisy in a final letter to the archbishop.

"One finds a loving, forgiving and caring God most easily when that God is manifest in a loving and caring Church. I have not found that to be forthcoming in our correspondence. I do not seek forgiveness from the Church since I believe that it is the Church that should be seeking forgiveness from me.

"I'd also like to address your comment that I am not being logical but emotional in my request. I wonder why you recently paid a half-million dollars to the victim of Father P but will do nothing to help me. Why did you settle that suit if you do not believe the Church owes restitution to those who are wronged by its agents?"

When she reads about the archbishop's own sexual misconduct in the newspaper, she realizes it is too late to save the prelate from his own folly.

# 54

"This thing with Sister Amelia and the Church just doesn't feel settled to me," Carole tells Dr. Bemmer while they share a cup of coffee in a local cafe. The two have become friends, and a leisurely breakfast is on today's agenda.

"Do you know what you are looking for?"

"Full disclosure I guess. Sister Amelia testified she 'fondled me' once. I stopped her fourth attempt when I detected sexual overtones in what she was doing. I was really angry at her. I accused her of manipulating me. I though what she was doing was a legitimate therapy practice. I let her know I was now in control and she would never get away with something like that again. Things were never the same between us after that."

She brushes a tear away and clears her throat. "Her behavior wasn't just the momentary slip on her part as she implied. It was done with forethought and intent. She brought a stool into the therapy room that wasn't there the first time I came."

"I applaud you for confronting her," Bemmer responds. "That took a lot of courage," she adds, placing her hand on Carole's arm.

Not sure where this conversation is going, Carole stares out the window through the dense fog that hangs over the city. She can scarcely make out the corner traffic lights blinking stop and go and caution, but she knows from the intermittent traffic flow that they're operational.

"Back in the 1950's and early 60's," she reminisces, "the Church recruited thirteen-year-old kids for the convents and minor seminaries. We should have grown up in a home, not an institution. Being separated from our families and friends was not a good thing."

The arrival of their breakfast order temporarily disrupts the conversation. Scrambled eggs, bacon, pancakes on the side, and a conscientious waitress who fills their half-empty cups. The chitter-chatter of the Saturday morning crowd crescendos. Families and friends are enjoying a day free from the stress of the workweek. The sharing of neighborhood news, intimate conversations, and the giggles of little children take precedence over the muted TV commentary on world events.

Once the waitress moves away, Carole continues to describe life in the aspiranture. "High School and we had no access to newspapers or radio or magazines or telephones. We never went to town. We were pretty lonely and vulnerable, isolated as we were from family and friends. We were even discouraged from talking to the day students who attended classes with us. They were outsiders, too 'dangerous' for us, I guess."

"What you're telling me sounds almost cult-like," Bemmer notes, "but surely you could make friends in the convent?"

"The nuns were always watching for cliques. They called them 'particular friendships.' Anyone who pursued a best friend would just disappear in the night. We'd discover an empty desk or bed the next day. No explanation given. We all understood they'd been sent home."

"Best friends fuel connection, something humans need," Bemmer replies. "Especially at that age. Without it, all kind of bad things can happen. I can see why you might be angry at Sister Amelia, but she's not responsible for all the rest of that."

"No, it was the institution, not just her. I was just trying to help you understand what was going on. Even the order recognized how destructive that early underage recruitment was. Eventually they stopped it."

Moving her plate aside for the waitress to pick it up, she modifies her anger. "Not to be too negative, I still appreciate many things about the convent. I can't forget the good education I got there. And I do appreciate that Sister Amelia testified for me."

It's clear to Dr. Bemmer that Carole is still locked in a love-hate relationship with the order. In psychobabble, the imbalance she is experiencing would be called *cognitive dissonance*. The growing noise in the café is not conducive to any further discussion here. She summons the waitress for the check.

"My treat," Bemmer offers. Wanting to offer something more, she volunteers, "Maybe we could set up a meeting with Sister Amelia and Mother Superior sometime? The convent was once family for you. I understand how it hurts that things ended the way they did. You need closure. Maybe a person-to-person conversation would be healing?"

"I'd like that, but I never want to be in the same room with them alone."

"You don't have to be alone anymore, Carole. How about I set up a meeting with the four of us? Call me with a contact number and we'll go from there."

Dr. Bemmer looks at her watch. "I have to go now, and you're due at work soon."

While pacing in Dr. Bemmer's waiting room, Carole scarcely notices the neon lights flickering on as dusk settles in the commercial downtown district. Or the piercing sound of the fog horn. She's too busy trying to focus her racing thoughts. Bemmer helped her do that last time they met. Now if she could just remember what they talked about.

Uppermost, she wants answers. Why didn't Mother Superior ever ask to hear her side of the story? Why such indifference? Why did she write, "When you left, you signed a paper stating you would not hold us responsible for anything"? Did she really think that included sexual abuse? Didn't she realize that Carole was only 23 at the time, in crisis, and had no idea what she was signing?

Carole hears the psychiatrist moving about in her inner office. She smells fresh brewing coffee and her dry mouth begins to salivate. She glances at the clock. How much longer? Time has been dragging all day. Like Janus, her mind has been leaping forward, then glancing back at ghost images from the 1950's.

*At twelve going on thirteen, I have to select an appropriate high school. I want to follow my older sister into the convent so I write to the order for information on how to apply to the aspiranture. Recruitment information arrives swiftly.*

*I still have it, here in my pocket. Mom saved it.*

*The brochure promises I can be a Bride of Christ. Wow. What an honor! But it warns I have to respond quickly before the allure of the world pulls me away. Whatever that means.*

*One Sunday the priest cautions parents from the pulpit. "Don't interfere in a child's call to a religious vocation." That seals it. My parents give their reluctant consent for me to go. Little do they know that life inside the convent holds its own dangers. Neither do I.*

Called back to the present by a phone jingling in the psychiatrist's inner office, Carole hears muffled voices. The office door opens. "That was a call from Sister Amelia," Dr. Bemmer announces. "They're going to be late. Mother Superior is tied up in a meeting."

Carole feels her tension mounting. "They're not backing out, are they? They wouldn't do that?"

"No, no," the doctor assures her. "Just a delay. I can hang around. I've plenty to do here—a few calls to make and a report that's due in court tomorrow. Can you find something to keep you busy?"

"No problem," Carole replies. "I'll do some writing," she says, pencil and notebook in hand.

"Here's a thought," Bemmer suggests. "Journal. What do you hope to accomplish in this meeting? Need any coffee, tea, or soda while you're waiting?"

"I'm okay. Thanks anyway. It would help if I had something to write on, though."

Bemmer leaves and returns with a large clipboard, then retreats to her inner office.

Carole breathes deeply, then begins jotting down her scattered thoughts. As time passes, her concerns take shape. She realizes that with Dr. Bemmer here to moderate, the door is open for an honest conversation. All parties have a right to be heard. This being a therapy clinic and not a courtroom, whatever is shared is confidential.

A second phone call interrupts Carole's writing. Muffled voices again. She crosses her fingers so tightly they begin to hurt. If she could cross her toes, she'd do that too. When Bemmer opens the door, the look on her face says the news is not good.

The psychiatrist clears her throat, walks over to the window where darkness has settled in. She attempts to recover a measure of professional objectivity, but can't. She's angry and upset. Allowing herself time to cool down, she finally turns to face Carole.

"I'm sorry, Sister Amelia and Mother Assumption aren't coming after all," she sighs. "They just lawyered up."

Carole bites her lower lip to hold back sobs. She rips the pages from her notebook, tears them into shreds. Silence shrouds the room. There are no words.

Eventually, like Bemmer, Carole regains her composure. She scribbles something across the cover of her notebook, then holds it up for the psychiatrist to read—the words of the poet William Ernest Henley: "I am the master of my fate, I am the Captain of my soul."

"Thanks for trying, Dr. Bemmer," she mumbles. She pulls herself tall as she prepares to leave. "They won't keep me in prison forever. I won't let them. I'll find my way past this. I've done all I can for now. It's time to put this aside. I've got a family to raise."

The therapy office door closes behind her.

# 55

Curious about the status of the medical board's appeal to the state supreme court, Carole scans the local newspaper for articles about the attorney general. One night, she reads the man is in hot water for his philandering, something that does not bode well either for the politician or for her case.

She reminds herself it's not really her case anymore—it belongs to the state; but somehow, it still feels personal. The state needs legal clarification on whether the statute of limitations should be applied to cases of professional malfeasance. Does the passage of time curtail their ability to take disciplinary action?

She calls Abe Friedman after she learns that the attorney general resigned under pressure. Her gut tells her this will impact their case. She's right, the lawyer admits. The AG's resignation sounds a death knell for their case that just expired in his to-do box.

"It can't have been all for nothing," she sighs as she shares her frustration with Arvid over this latest disappointment. "Nothing much more I can do now. It's over."

"That's not like you," he says. "How about writing to the assistant attorney general? See what he has to say."

Carole follows his advice. She receives this response.

"Regrettable as it is, the court system does not in fact always secure justice; it is, however, our only chance for justice. When letters like yours arrive, it necessarily requires an examination of the entire system to see what might be done in the future to prevent the pain and suffering that people in your situation have needlessly sustained."

*But if healing is not to be found in the courtroom, where else should I look?* she asks herself. She files that question along with his letter in the lockbox of her heart, hoping to address it someday in the future.

# *Epilogue*

Hope is being able to see that there is light despite all the darkness.

— Desmond Tutu

Victims of sexual trauma are prone to PTSD (post-traumatic stress disorder) but many move on to PTG (post-traumatic growth.) Confronting the abuse and the abuser is a first step in that direction. When they network with fellow survivors and supporters, they gain strength, knowing they are not alone. To protect others from similar abuse, they may engage in consciousness-raising and advocate for better oversight. Eventually, they may even find a deeper spiritual life, following the advice Nelson Mandela delivered after his years in imprisonment. "When a deep injury is done to us, we never heal until we forgive."

Closing time at the heavenly courthouse, and everyone's vacating the place at once. Themis wishes she had taken a different corridor when she spots Justice coming down the hall towards her. That Roman babe loves to gloat when she wins, and the goddess does not feel up to dealing with such arrogance right now.

As the two approach each other, Themis ungraciously admits defeat. "You won," she grumbles. She's taken aback by what transpires next. "What? No gloating? You looked utterly crushed, Justice. What gives?"

"Nobody really won," she mumbles. She rips off her blindfold and shields her eyes against a light that is almost more than she can bear. Then she wails angrily, "This was never a fair fight. Something's got to change."

"That's what I've been saying for centuries!" Themis reminds her. "Nobody listens." She doubles over in pain, clutches her belly. The ulcer's acting up again. She'd like to swear, but that would be way too ungodly. "With that mandate from the gods, we can't intervene. Our hands are tied. It's up to humans to work things out. They've got the tools, if they'd only use them. Head, heart, free will. What more do they need?"

Justice has the saddest look on her face. Putting aside their philosophical differences, Themis offers her comfort. "Remember Carole's dream about the snowball?" she says, wrapping her arms around her compatriot's shoulder.

She nods.

"That snowball can become an avalanche. Carole's case and others like it are the rumblings that precede an approaching avalanche. I foresee others will step forward someday to admit 'me too'. Nothing will stop the movement that will follow."

"So you're telling me the story isn't over yet?"

"I am."

Themis pauses. After due consideration of the whole picture, she changes her original perspective. "I don't think Carole lost at all. She never found the justice she was seeking, but she found many friends and supporters who helped on her journey. She's become stronger than she ever was before. Can't knock that, Justice. Can't take it away from her, either. Given a passage of time, I predict she will discover the path to ultimate healing."

"What's that?" Justice inquires.

"Why, the best way to recover from a serious injury is to forgive the offender. Forgiveness is a difficult but rewarding choice. It may take years, hard work, and the help of a very special friend to ever reach that milestone. I think she's got the motivation to take that final step."

"I'll bet on Carole this time 'round," Justice responds in a more positive tone, then gives Themis a sisterly hug.

"Me, too."

# To Contact the Author

You can connect with Becky at:

www.astatutewithlimitations.com

a website committed to providing a welcoming platform where sur-vivors of therapist and counselor abuse are not silenced by the statute of limitations. Family and friends are welcome to visit as well.